THE
WAGER

Other books by Carolyn Brown:

The *Promised Land Romance* Series:

Willow
Velvet
Gyspy
Garnet
Augusta

The *Land Rush Romance* Series:

Emma's Folly
Violet's Wish
Maggie's Mistake
Just Grace

Love Is
A Falling Star
All the Way from Texas
The Yard Rose
The Ivy Tree
Lily's White Lace
That Way Again

THE
WAGER

•

Carolyn Brown

AVALON BOOKS
NEW YORK

With love to Mischelle, Sarah, and Beth.

Prologue

"I don't care if he's the king of France and can lay the Hope diamond at my feet, I don't want to meet him right now. He's a spoiled brat of a man, I already know that just from what I've heard. So give it up, Daddy. I'll work with him but I damn sure don't have to like him," Ivy Cameo Marshall straightened the lapel of her silk Italian tailored suit and glared at her father over the top of a gleaming mahogany desk.

"You're going to be working with him every day in just a month, Ivy. We'd like to know if you two are going to clash before hand so we can make other arrangements," Red said.

"I can work with Lucifer if I have to," Ivy said. "Especially after a whole month in the south of France, lying on the beach and shopping."

"Poor little rich girl," her junior associate and best friend, Joyce, tucked a strand of blond hair behind her ear.

"Don't you start that with me," Ivy wiggled her finger

at Joyce. "Just because you choose to spend your vacation in some tiny little town up in Oklahoma, don't berate me because I choose to spend mine being spoiled."

"You are spoiled," Joyce said. "Girl, you wouldn't last three days in the working class population. If you had to run the Strawberry Moon like I do every summer so my sister and her family can go to Mexico on their church mission work, you'd collapse in a day."

Red chuckled. "You got that right, Joyce. Thank goodness she doesn't have to do that kind of work. The world would come to an end if Ivy ever had to waitress for a living and give up her eel briefcase and designer suits. Or worse yet, if she had to do her own laundry."

Ivy turned her back on both of them. She could run that burger joint standing on her head and cross eyed. Lord Almighty, she'd been running the Dallas Oil Company, at least the financial end of it, for more than five years. Granted she had lots of qualified help in the way of well educated and trained staff, and she'd be lost without Joyce. But what was a burger joint in Davis, Oklahoma compared to a huge firm like the oil company?

"What're you going to do these next four weeks?" Joyce ignored her friend's pouting and asked Red.

"Work," Red ran his fingers through thick deep red hair with just the faintest sprinkling of gray beginning in his temples. "I'm going on to Austin and get the basic things polished up so when we open the doors of the new company, it'll run like a greased machine. I just wish Ivy would reconsider and come home a couple of days early to meet the other vice president."

"Don't you lay a guilt trip on me," Ivy spun around. "I told you I can work with this Will Dalhart. I don't have to meet him before hand. He'll keep his business and his ego on the third floor in production. I'll keep mine on the fourth floor and pay for drilling and hopefully not too many of his mistakes."

"I'll hold you to it," Red said. "Don't you come whining to me that you can't stand to be in the same room with the man. Personally, I think he's a fine fellow. Smart as they come and can literally smell oil. I can count on one finger the number of times he's hit a dry hole."

"Well, by all means let's don't ever let him catch a cold," Ivy said. "Joyce, will you call the airline and confirm my flight out at ten tomorrow morning, please?"

"I'll do it," Joyce said. "And while you are baking all that white skin you can think of me making burgers in Oklahoma when what I really want to do is join April and her family on the mission trip to Mexico. Just one time I want to go with them and help with building a new addition on the church or a house for some poor family rather than staying home in an air conditioned cafe and playing at waitressing. It's just that there's no one to run the Strawberry Moon if I do."

"Oh, stop your whining," Ivy checked her makeup in a gold compact and reapplied her lipstick. "You could be going to France with me and you know it. It's your choice to run that cafe. They could close it for a month in the summer rather than keeping it open."

"I bet you couldn't do it, so don't tell me to stop whining," Joyce said. Thank goodness she and Ivy had been friends since kindergarten. She couldn't imagine talking to a boss like that, but a friend was a different matter.

"Oh, I could too," Ivy said.

"Prove it," Joyce said.

"You mean you are serious about wanting me to go up there to that little town and run a cafe instead of going to France?" Ivy asked incredulously.

"Bet you can't do it. Bet you'll fold in two days and I'll have to come home from Mexico and bail you out. Bet you can't live on a minimum wage salary for a month and do the work of a waitress and cafe manager," Joyce taunted.

"I could too, but I'm not going to. That's the single craziest bet you've every thrown at me," Ivy smiled.

"I'll bet you can't," Red said. "I'll bet you a brand new Caddy with all the extras."

Ivy stared at both of them. They were crazy as outhouse rats. Surely they'd been dipping into the bourbon all morning to even suggest such a thing.

"And I'll bet," Joyce touched her cheek in deep thought, "I'll bet . . ."

"You've both been out in the sun too long. Your brains are fried," Ivy said with half a giggle. She could buy a new Caddy and never miss the money, so why was she thinking about how many options she could order at her father's expense? "And if I were to take this fool bet, what would happen if I didn't last? If I was mature enough after a week to admit I could not do it?"

"You forfeit the Caddy and you have to come to Austin and help me instead of going to France," Red said.

"Or if you can't run a cafe, then you have to come to Mexico and help me do mission work and I'll send my sister home," Joyce said.

"And what do I get from you if I do win?" She asked Joyce.

"A whole week in December. I'll cover for you to go to France or wherever you want. I'll do your work as well as mine and keep things in good standing," Joyce told her.

She could prolong her trip to France until December. She'd have to forget tanning on the beach, but it would be a welcome change after several months of getting a company through the first throes of birth. Great heavens, what was she thinking? True, she'd always had a problem with challenges, but to give up four weeks in France to work as a waitress? Her brain must be fried crisp as an apple tart—not theirs.

"Rules?" She asked.

"The cafe is open six days a week. You'll have to run it single handedly except for hiring a short order cook. That's what I do every summer. If you can find one to work twelve hours a day that's fine. Or you can hire two. April's already got an ad running in the local paper to replace the lady who's cooking now. Should be a dozen kids begging for a summer job when they see the ad. Rule is you can't leave Murray County. That way you can't come running back to Dallas for a bit of big city life on Sundays when the cafe is closed. You got any more rules, Red?" Joyce asked.

"You have to leave behind your computer, cell phone, and wardrobe. Pick up some jeans and tee shirts to work in," Red said. If that didn't stop his daughter in her tracks nothing ever would.

"You have to live in the double wide trailer where I was going to live. The master bedroom has a private bathroom and it's a really nice place to live but it's sure not what you are used to. Only thing is the dryer's broken, but there are clothes lines out back. And just to make it interesting, you can't have the dryer fixed," Joyce added.

"Anything else? Do I have to scrub floors or only have one bath a week? Do I get to take my toothbrush?" Ivy asked sarcastically.

"No, that's about it, except you do have to mop floors at the cafe. I'll make up a list of things you'll have to do. Like when the produce man delivers and when the frozen food vendor comes. I'll make it as easy on you as I can," Joyce said, expecting Ivy to back down any minute.

"Any color Caddy I want?" Ivy eyed Red, expecting him to retract his bet.

"Name it," Red grinned, knowing fully well he'd never have to buy a Caddy. His spoiled daughter wouldn't last thirty minutes in a situation like that, much less thirty days.

"Then you are both on. I'm sick of you two thinking I'm nothing but a brat. I'll show you and don't you be calling me in December whining and carrying on about the work load when I'm off in Switzerland on the ski slopes," she frowned at Joyce.

"Or you when I order a Caddy that will make your checking account bawl like a baby," she told her father.

"Pack your bags tonight then, honey, because tomorrow we drive to Davis, Oklahoma. And the next morning I leave on the church bus with my family to go to Mexico," Joyce clapped her hands.

An idea took hold of Red's mind like a hungry hound with a soup bone. "Oh, one more thing. You have to use a different name, Ivy. I don't know that folks up there would recognize you from the pictures on the fronts of magazines and in the Dallas newspapers, but you can't be letting people know you're the rich kid. Let's say you go by your middle name, Cameo, and your mother's maiden name, Johnson. How's that?"

"Fine with me," Ivy said. "From this point on I am Cameo Johnson, the waitress and manager of the Strawberry Moon hamburger joint in Davis, Oklahoma."

John William Dalhart had just finished his last meeting with the board of directors in Houston, Texas. Now he was officially on vacation. Tomorrow he'd be off on a well deserved and long awaited month of relaxation. After that, it would be nose to the grindstone getting the new company up and going. He'd approved of the merger with Dallas Oil Company when his father brought him the idea. He'd liked the notion of a new building in Austin, and had been honored when he met with his father and Red Marshall and the two of them asked him to head up the production end of the new business. He wasn't real happy with their plan of putting Red's daughter in the position of co-vice-president in charge of finances, but that was a minor detail. He could work with a woman, as long as she kept on her floor and didn't interfere in his business. He just hoped she wasn't some ditzy blond who was only glorified window dressing.

"So where you off to?" his father asked from the other side of the empty office. Boxes lined the walls. Each neatly labeled and ready to be moved to Austin.

"Somewhere exotic, you can be sure," Red Marshall said. "South of France?"

"Nothing that exotic," Will smiled, his grin deepening the deep dimples in his cheeks. "I've got tentative plans to go to New York for a couple of weeks. See a Broadway play, look up some old college buddies who are in the publishing business. Then make up my mind where I'm going after that."

"Kids today," Red said with a flip of his hand. "We stay home and work to get the business settled in and running while they dash off and play."

"Is that what your daughter is doing? Dashing off to play?" Will asked, an antsy feeling in his chest telling him an ill wind was blowing through his office.

"Oh, to be sure," Red said, his blue eyes twinkling. "She mentioned the south of France. Off playing. You young people wouldn't know a thing about working like your father and I did forty years ago. Back when it was normal to work twenty out of twenty four hours."

Will smiled. Red must be really mad at his daughter for not giving up her time and helping get things underway in Austin. Thank goodness his father didn't see things in that light. A generous man, John Dalhart had always allowed time to play as well as work.

John Dalhart shook his head slowly, a gesture Will had seen many times. One that had always come right before a lecture when Will was a teenager. "Will's a fine young man, Red. He'll do his job well and he deserves a vacation. Just as much as your daughter, Ivy, does. I'd never expect him to give up his vacation time. I wouldn't want him to have to work at minimum wage like I did in the beginning of my working days. We've worked our whole lives to keep them from experiencing those horrible hard times," John chuckled.

"Oh?" Will narrowed his crystal clear blue eyes and scowled at them both.

"And what's that look on your face?" John asked. "I'm not saying you couldn't live on minimum wage or find a job for yourself. I'm just saying that you don't have to and I wouldn't expect you to. So don't raise your eyebrows at me like that. Go on to New York and come home refreshed and ready to work."

"You think I couldn't live on a minimum wage? You don't think I'd last a week without all the amenities and power money brings. You don't have to say it. It's written all over both of your faces." He said coldly.

"Truth is, I don't think you could, but it's not important. The important thing is that you don't have to," John said.

"I bet I could," Will said.

"What you willing to bet?" Red narrowed his eyes.

"What are you two willing to bet?" He asked.

Red rubbed his chin, "How about a fancy new sports car?"

"Why would you spring for something that big?" Will asked, narrowing his own blue eyes.

"Because I can," Red said.

"Oh, humor us," John said. "We're having a bit of fun here, Will. It's just a wager that we won't hold you to. But if we were betting for real, I'd be willing to bet that horse you been badgering me about that you won't last a month out there in the blue collar world."

"You'd put Five Track on the line for a silly bet like this?" Will asked.

"I don't imagine I'd be losing Five Track, but this has gone on far enough. It's gotten out of hand. You're not serious about betting, are you?" His father asked. "Besides, what would you lay on the line if you lost?"

"I wouldn't lose, but the point is moot. I'm going to New York, not staying in Dallas to work at sweeping out McDonald's."

"Oh, you couldn't stay in Dallas," Red said. "Too many folks would know you. You'd have to be an unknown drifter looking for work."

"This is ridiculous," Will laughed uneasily. To be branded someone who couldn't hold down a menial job was sticking in his craw.

"You'd have to get out of the state so no one would possibly know you and you'd have to chose a fake name too," his father said. "You could use Sonny and get yourself one of those temporary tattoos like you did in college that about gave your mother a full fledged heart attack."

"And which state do I have to live in? What other rules are there to proving myself a man?" A frigid chill filling the room from his voice.

"Oh, Oklahoma would be fine," his father said. "Just over the border even. But it couldn't be a big city where you could have Broadway plays. It would have to be just a small town, but why are we even discussing this craziness? Go on back to your apartment and finish getting ready for your flight tomorrow."

"How far into Oklahoma would you suggest?" Will asked. He'd show them both, and he'd choose the most expensive car on the market at the end of a month.

"Right over the border is a town called Ardmore, but that's too big," Red said, pretending to be thinking.

"Next one of any size at all on Interstate 35 is a little place called Davis. Home of Turner Falls Park. Went up there a few years ago to see about buying some oil leases but changed my mind. There used to be a man living up there who had a nose for oil almost as good as yours. Town has got about three thousand of the friendliest people in the whole state. There's a nice Main Street and at least one grocery store. Maybe you could find employment as a checker or sacker."

"Yeah, right," Will said.

"I stopped in at a little cafe when I was up there. Must've been twenty years ago now. The Strawberry Moon, it was called. Famous for its grilled onion burger. You could eat there when you didn't want to cook for yourself. On minimum wage you won't be going out to eat much, though. It'd be a real treat to get an onion burger once a week. By the time you pay for a place to live and normal expenses you won't have a surplus to be spending on expensive dining," Red said.

"I'll take your wagers," Will declared.

"Ah, son, don't be silly, we were just joking with you," John said. "No one doubts your ability to work. You're the best in the field. Come on now. Let's go on down to the club and order lunch."

"I'm doing it," Will clenched his jaw. "The only thing I'll take is my motorcycle and a couple of changes of clothes and a hundred dollars to get me a place to sleep until I get a pay check."

"No plastic?" Red asked. "I didn't know anyone under thirty could live without credit cards."

"Not even a three piece suit. Just some blue jeans and tee shirts," Will said. "And if I lose I'll put ten thousand dollars in your favorite charity. You can each choose whichever one you prefer. But if I win, I want the car, the horse, and another vacation in the winter. A whole week. My time and my choosing."

"Fair enough. I could run production a few days for you, but I'm not figuring on losing the bet," Red said.

"You sure you're up to this, son?" John asked, seriously.

"I'm damn sure. And don't you ever doubt me again," Will said.

"Well, then if you're that sure, let's throw in another little rule. You got to get some sweet little girl to say she'll marry you too," John laughed.

"Done," Will said.

"Forget it, Will. That time I was really just joking around. A month isn't long enough to fall in love and work too," John looked misty eyed. "Of course, I fell in love with your mother in less than a month. In the beginning I'd work all day and find time to take her a bouquet of wild flowers in the evening. Lord I miss that woman even after all these years. We were supposed to be married forever and die together. But like she said there at the end, she was just going on to get heaven ready for me. Guess it's taking a lot of getting ready for someone like me," John said.

"I can do it," Will told them. "I'll keep a journal and even bring you proof that some woman says she'll marry me. Now I'm going home to cancel a bunch of reservations and get ready to show you two that men today are just as tough as they were in your day."

"That'll take some proving, son," John's eyes glittered with amusement.

"I can do it," Will turned back at the door and grinned for the first time. "What's the name of that place that serves those hamburgers? You have got my mouth watering for one."

"The Strawberry Moon. It probably isn't even there now. That was twenty years ago, Will, but if it is and they still make an onion burger, think of me when you're eating it," Red said.

"I'll see you in a month, Dad. Is it against the rules to call in?"

"No, you can call once a week, and I've got your cell phone number in case of an emergency," John said.

"Then it's a done deal," Will shut the door softly behind him.

"Well, that went off without a hitch," Red said when he was sure Will was really gone.

"Yes, it did. Now about our wager. You'll give me that prize bull I been trying to buy from you for a year if Will comes home before the month is finished," John said.

"Consider it done. And you'll give me that stud horse I have been trying to buy from you for two years if my girl comes home with a broken finger nail and carrying on about the work being too hard," Will said.

"That's what we said," John stuck out his hand and the two of them shook on the deal.

Chapter One

Cameo Johnson hated two things in this world. Cooking was both of them. Running a close third place was losing a bet. So the next person who walked through the door of the Strawberry Moon had better be looking for a job as a cook or else both her options involved anger. She could march her bone tired feet back to the kitchen and learn to make hamburgers and foot long hot dogs in the space of one afternoon. Or she could lose the bet.

Even if it meant cooking, she wasn't going to lose the bet.

Her nose pressed against the glass door of the Strawberry Moon cafe located a mile south of a little town called Davis in south central Oklahoma, she tried to conjure up an applicant for the job. Anyone would do! A high school sophomore, girl or boy, with a high pitched giggle, sporting a teenager's sense of humor or even whining about acne. A woman named Gert who wore Spandex pants and a tee shirt with Elvis on the front. Cameo didn't care, just so long as they were willing to work long hours at minimum wage. Like she'd told her father and best friend, she could work with Lucifer.

Looking back she had worked with lots of Lucifers and dated even more. At least the romances usually only lasted one date or maybe two if they thought they could endure the plain Jane woman to get to her father's bank account. Cameo might have been born blessed with wealth, brains, and opportunity, but somehow she got left out in the yard when it came to grace and luck in love.

She sighed and kept her vigil beside the door. Joyce said the ad had been running in the local paper for three weeks and was confident that by the time the cook fulfilled her week long notice there would be a dozen people standing in line for the job. Well, guess who was wrong? Again! She'd been wrong when she goaded Cameo into the bet, and she was darn sure wrong now. Nobody in Davis, Oklahoma wanted to cook hamburgers, hot-dogs, steak sandwiches, French fries, and make milk shakes all summer.

A wavy aura arose from the hot highway. Little curls of fluttering, pure old devil hot heat mesmerized Cameo in the middle of another sweltering afternoon. She pulled back away from the glass and rubbed the nose print away with the dish towel she carried constantly. After three days, she'd already learned more about how the other half lived than she'd thought possible. And now she was going to have to learn to cook, but by golly, she'd win this bet even if she had to be the bionic superwoman who ran the Strawberry Moon single-handedly for a month.

The sound of a motorcycle cut through the noise of the air conditioning unit kicking on, the scraping sound of the cook running a wide spatula over the grill as she cleaned it, and a lonesome cricket hiding somewhere, singing a solo. For a moment Cameo couldn't discern whether the cycle was coming into town from the south or leaving. She held her breath. If it was coming from town it was possible whoever was riding it might be looking for a job.

When she realized that it was coming from the wrong direction, she let the pent up breath out in a whoosh. The motorcycle and rider turned into the parking lot and she almost groaned. He wasn't a knight in shining armor and he hadn't come to carry her away on his big black Harley or to cook hamburgers in a tiny little kitchen, either. He was going to want one of the famous Strawberry Moon grilled onion burgers and he'd be on his way. No one who rode something that big and expensive would be looking for a job as a fry cook. He walked with confidence oozing out of him, moneyed without a doubt, in spite of the fact he was decked out in tight fitting jeans and a white tee shirt stretching over bulging muscles.

"Please tell me you are looking for a job as a cook," she said with a smile on her face when he opened the door.

He removed his helmet, shook out his perfectly cut dark brown hair and, eyed her carefully. Had he heard the woman right? Did she actually just offer him a job? Was he in Davis, Oklahoma?

"What did you say?" He asked, looking into the

greenest eyes he'd ever seen. Her strawberry blond hair was pulled back into a pony tail and sweat formed in little beads right above her upper lip. He half expected her to wipe it away with the sleeve of her pink tee shirt or the towel she had in her hand. Not a bad looking woman. Definitely not his type, though, with those glasses sliding down her sweaty nose.

"I said that I hope you're here looking for a job. I need a short order cook. Mine is leaving tomorrow," she said. "Have a seat. As you can well see, this is a slow time of the day. Menus are on the table. I'll be right with you. What can I get you to drink?"

"Tea, no sugar," he said. "You serious about needing a cook? Am I near Davis, Oklahoma?"

"Yes, I am and yes you are," she said.

"I've never cooked before," he said. "I'm just drifting around. Staying about a month in each place. Couldn't promise you anymore than that. And you'd have to give me some training."

"You serious?" She asked. Merciful heavens, he didn't look like a cook. With that big machine sitting out there, those brand new creased jeans, and the way he carried himself, he looked more like he'd just walked out of an advertisement for high dollar whiskey. That didn't even take into consideration the expensive new shoes he had on his feet that hadn't seen a mile's usage yet. He could be a serial killer just turned loose from prison, especially with that jail house tattoo on his muscular upper arm advertising for the whole world that he was Sonny.

"I might be," he flashed a smile, showing off even white teeth.

He couldn't be an ex-con. Not with teeth like that. Didn't all ex-convicts have their two front teeth knocked out and the ones on either side of the gap decayed or tobacco stained?

"But I want that tea and to eat first while I think about it," he said. His heart was beating double time. He had barely made it to Davis and already he had the prospect of a job. He didn't care if it was nothing more than a cook in a two-bit restaurant that smelled like grease and fried onions. A job was a job. That alone was half of his commitment.

Cameo delivered his tea and waited beside the booth for him to look at the menu. "The onion burgers are the specialty. Folks come from all over the county to get them."

"Then that's what I'll have," he said.

"Fries?" She asked, not even writing down the order. Even with her limited abilities she could remember one order.

"No. Got baked potatoes?" He asked.

She laughed. "You eat fries with your onion burgers. Baked potatoes come with steak, but we don't serve that here. You'd have to go on up the road to get a steak. There's a small restaurant on the west side of the highway called the 77 Grill. You might get a baked potato there or a steak. I haven't been there myself, just know that it's there. Then there's a couple of places just off Main, turn left at the red light. They might have that kind of food," she laughed. "But this is the official burger joint that serves fries and burgers. It's the redneck cafe."

You can say that again, and you're a redneck honey if I ever saw one, he thought. All of his brand new cheap clothes would be too tight by the end of the month if he ate fries every day.

"Then just the onion burger and while I eat you can tell me about this job," he said. "You own this place?"

At least he talked proper for a man who'd just put in his time in prison, she thought. Probably in one of those low security places for laundering money for the mob rather than in solitary confinement for murder. She conjured up a vision of Don Corleone and his son Michael. Even if the stranger looked nothing like Michael, he could be a modern day mobster.

"No, I'm the manager, at least for the next few weeks," she said.

"And what do you do when you're not managing the Strawberry Moon?" He glanced down at the menu and still couldn't believe his eyes. Who in their right mind would name a restaurant something so corny?

"Not much," she crossed her fingers behind her back. "Just odd jobs. I manage to stay busy. I'm doing this as a favor for my . . . for a friend."

"I understand," he nodded. "Is the Strawberry Moon some kind of fancy ice cream dessert you serve here?"

She grinned. "I asked the exact same question. No, we just serve shakes and ice cream cones. Not even sundaes. A strawberry moon, they tell me, is the name of a full moon in June. There was some inside story about the owner's grandparents who were the original owners of the place. They never told the whole story, just that a strawberry moon was very important to them so that's what they named the place. Be right back," she said, going through the swinging doors beside the cash register sitting on the top of a short bar with a glass showcase of candy bars beneath it. She gave the cook the order and hurried back, half expecting to see nothing but the back end of the Harley lighting a shuck for anywhere but the Strawberry Moon. Not even someone with a rap sheet a yard long would want to work the hours she was about to tell him about.

"So sit down and tell me about this job," he motioned for her to slide into the booth across from him.

"I'm looking for a cook from nine in the morning to nine at night. If you're a drifter and don't want to worry with W-2 forms later, I'll pay you in cash money and call it contract labor," she said. "No taxes. No records." If that didn't tempt him nothing would. To win this bet, she'd pay him out of her own money.

"Why would you do that?" He asked.

"I need a cook very badly. You need a job. We can cover it as contract labor and you won't have to worry with another W-2 form trying to find its way to you," she said. Maybe this wasn't such a good idea after all. Could be he was a tax man prowling around looking for a reason to haul her tired rear end to the jail down on Main Street.

"It doesn't matter how you pay me. Cash is fine if I take the job, but I'll take a check and leave you an address for the tax forms to be mailed. I do have a permanent address I can use," he said.

"Are you a convict?" She asked bluntly.

"No, I'm in the witness protection program for the next month," he laughed.

"For real?" Her eyes widened.

"No, I'm lying," he said. "I'm just a drifter."

"Order!" The cook yelled from the kitchen and

Cameo jumped up, telling him on the way out of the dining area that she needed a cook twelve hours a day.

"You really expect someone to work those kind of hours?" He asked when she set the platter before him.

"I didn't until today. I really need two cooks. We're open from nine in the morning to nine at night, but you're the only one who's been interested in working."

"That's twelve hour days," he said, dreading being cooped up in a kitchen that many hours every day.

"Yes, it is," she nodded. "I'd thought I'd be swamped with applicants. So did the owner when she left three days ago. We figured we could hire two cooks for six hour shifts. But I haven't been swamped and you're the only person I could even interest in the job."

"Starting when?"

"Right now," she winced. "The cook can train you all afternoon and you'd be on your own tomorrow."

"Minimum wage?" He asked.

She nodded.

"Deal, then. Got a suggestion where I could rent a room?"

She shook her head. "There are three motels in town I think. A couple you would've passed on back down the highway. Another one closer to Main Street going into town. Cabins everywhere," she looked at him long and serious. At the rate the motels charged he'd barely make enough to pay for his room working for minimum wage. If he really was in the witness protection program he wouldn't do anything to jeopardize his position, and he'd acted pretty glib when he'd volunteered that information, almost as if he were really telling the truth, yet making it appear to be a joke.

"I'm staying in the owner's house back behind the cafe here. It's actually a double wide trailer with three bedrooms. I've got the master bedroom with the private bath and a lock on the door. Just thought I'd let you know that up front about the lock since I don't know you from any other serial killer. You probably are in the witness protection program or you wouldn't know so much about it. I'd rent you either of the kids' rooms. Both are girl's rooms. Pink walls, lace curtains, and teddy bears on the shelves. Fifty dollars a week. Any food you eat here is free. Anything you want at the house, you buy and fix for yourself," she said.

"How many days a week?"

"Work or rent?"

"Both," he said.

"Six days a week for the work. Seven for the rent. The dryer is broken but the clothes lines work fine. You do your own laundry and clean up after yourself. I don't pick up dirty socks and I don't cook for you. There's a carport where you can park the Harley. I walk to work since it's only a couple of blocks. You can do what you please. Davis has less than three thousand people so if you're looking for night life after you get off work, you're fresh out of luck. That is if you've got the energy to go looking at anything after twelve hours in the kitchen."

"Deal," he said. "Sundays off?"

"That's right. My friend and her family don't open on Sunday. That's the official day of rest," Cameo told him.

"And your name, boss lady?" He bit into the onion burger and rolled his eyes in appreciation. It was absolutely scrumptious.

"I'm Cameo Johnson, and you are?" She pointed toward the black tattoo done in a fine script lettering.

"John," he stammered, on the verge of blurting out his real name. "Johnson, Sonny Johnson," he said. "Guess we got the same last name, but it's about the most common name there is in the phone book next to Williams. No past, so don't ask me. I'm only interested in today, so don't go boring me about my long term future plans either," he told her. "I'll finish this and then scuttle back through those doors for my hands on training in the field of culinary arts."

She didn't like him. Not one bit. He was too smooth and much, much too sure of himself. Witness protection for what? She wondered. She'd be willing to bet her job in Austin at the end of the month that his real name was John something and he'd just covered his mistake. However, he would work seventy two hours a week for minimum wage. Which would be just under four hundred dollars. At least he was willing to take a check and it wouldn't have to come out of her personal banking account.

And he would pay her fifty dollars a week to stay in the house. She'd leave the rent money in an envelope for Joyce to do with whatever she pleased. There was no way Cameo was going to have her friend and associate saying she'd made a profit from the bet.

"That your real name?" She asked, cold shivers dancing up her spine in spite of the summer heat. What on earth had she just done? Hired a man with a jail house tattoo and an attitude she didn't even like and even offered to let him live with her in the trailer. If she'd been at a five hundred dollar a plate political dinner and he'd been across the room, she wouldn't have given him the second glance. But then she didn't normally look twice at the hired help and even with the motorcycle, he was still just a drifter.

"No, but it will do for now. The witness protection program gives us new names and identities. And this is the best burger I've ever put in my mouth," he said.

"Thank you. April's been cooking them the same way for years according to my friend, Joyce, who is her sister. No wonder our tax dollars are so high if the WP program is buying Harley's for their witnesses," she smarted off, grabbing the bottle of window cleaner and going to work on the door. Men and kids! Neither one knew why doors were designed with handles. They slapped their greasy little unwashed palms on the glass and pushed. No wonder April bought glass cleaner in five gallon jugs.

Sonny was a quick study in the small kitchen area. Using an order pad, he tore sheets off and labeled the various places where he could find burger, steak and chicken patties, corn dogs, both regular length and foot long hot dogs. By the time the supper rush hit at just after five o'clock he and the cook were putting out orders fast enough to keep Cameo wearing out shoe leather running back and forth.

To Sonny it was only a different variation of a file cabinet. Label what you might need later, remember a few details like five minutes to do fries, two pulls on the handle to steam hot dog buns, watch the burger buns carefully on the grill so they didn't burn on the edges, slice the tomatoes thin, chop the lettuce fine, grill the onions just until they were semi-soft. By nine o'clock he felt like he'd played tennis all afternoon and lost every game, but he had the basics down. The cook had even shown him how to thoroughly clean the grill. Grease, too; telling Sonny that when the grease was old the fries came up soggy instead of crisp, the chicken and steak patties were limp and greasy. Grease had to be changed every third day, religiously.

Just as the normal supper rush thinned out, a tour bus parked outside the Strawberry Moon with more than thirty people unloading. The cafe was the first eating place off Interstate Highway 35 going toward town so every so often Cameo got a load of tourists, but that night she'd just as soon had a quiet evening. The profits would look good, but her feet were already aching.

She clothes-pinned the paper orders to the twine above the grill and took orders as fast as she could write, with one ear trained toward the kitchen to hear when either the older cook or Sonny yelled, "Order!"

People raised their voices above the juke box pumping out country western music. Tomorrow she promised herself she'd find the volume control and turn it down a notch or two. One cowboy bellied up to the video game in the back corner, plugged in his quarters, and added the pinging noise of a digital pin ball machine to the melee. Between trips to the kitchen, Cameo watched him play. He'd lean this way and that, wiggle his hips, hitch up his jeans with the inside edge of his wrists, and rotate his shoulders, trying to get the ball to follow his body language.

"Come on, let's dance to this one," one of the ladies approached him when the game finally ended. "Our order is the last one. We got time to dance."

"I don't dance," he said.

Cameo chuckled.

"What's so funny?" He asked.

"You don't dance? You been cutting a pretty good rug over there in front of that pin ball machine. Just pretend you're playing the game," Cameo pushed her glasses up on her nose.

"Why, thank you honey," the lady said. "He does have a fine little fanny, don't he? And the way it was moving made my old heart beat right fast. Now come on Buddy, dance with me."

"Thanks a lot," he sighed at Cameo good naturedly. "See what you got me into."

"So do you dance?" Sonny asked as he delivered half a dozen burger baskets to the front.

"No questions," Cameo shook her finger at him. "Remember, no past. No future." If that's the way he wanted it then she could play by the same rules. Matter of fact, she rather liked those rules.

He grinned. "Fair enough."

She called the number on the top of the ticket as she sat them on the counter beside the register and rang up the charges. By the time the bus reloaded, she barely had enough energy left to slap the closed sign in the window and lock the doors, and there were floors yet to mop.

The cook collected a last pay check and disappeared out the door before Cameo could ask for help with the final evening chores. Sonny leaned against the door jamb into the kitchen, watching Cameo pour cleaner into the galvanized bucket and fetch the big, industrial sized mop from the hook in the utility room. She wasn't comfortable with the job, that was as plain. He wondered for the thousandth time since he took the job just what she did when she wasn't managing cafes for her friends. Maybe some kind of exotic dancer with those long legs and nice body. If he squinted and looked real hard, there was some beauty hiding behind those thick-lensed glasses. Perhaps a little makeup would help. Hopefully she wasn't someone who'd shoot a fry cook in his sleep for his motorcycle. She'd mentioned a lock on her bedroom door. He hoped there was one on his as well.

"Here let me help with that. You look like you're ready to cave in. Did your last job not demand as many hours or as much labor?" He asked, dipping the mop and stomping the lever that wrung the water from the long off-white cotton strands.

"One more time, Sonny Johnson, no past and no questions," she answered, taking the mop from him and swishing it around the dirty, utilitarian, green tile floor.

"Sounds good to me," he grinned. "Got another one of those evil looking things? I can't go home tonight until you do. I'm tired and in need of a long, hot shower, so if I help then we can go faster."

"There's another one hanging in the utility room," she nodded in that direction.

Wordlessly, they worked until the job was finished and the floor sparkling clean, then he walked beside her, pushing the cycle rather than riding it. He parked it in the carport beside a Lexus. He raised an eyebrow at the car, but didn't ask. No past and no questions. Evidently Cameo Johnson didn't always work as a waitress. Either that or the tips were mighty good at the Strawberry Moon.

"It's not a big place," she said, marching tiredly across the redwood deck and up to the front door. She dug around in the bottom of her purse for the key. "This is the living room," she swung the door open and switched on the overhead lights.

Comfortable. A deep cushioned sofa on one wall. Full book cases on two walls. Plain brown carpet—well worn, needing replacement. Kitchen off to one side. Six chairs around a wooden table. *Family occupied* written all over everything.

"I've got the master bedroom. You can have this one," she led him down the hall. "It's closest to the bathroom."

He nodded. What could he say? That it would be fine? That was evident. That he loved it? That would be the most blatant lie he'd ever told. He plopped his duffel bag down on the twin bed. How long had it been since he'd slept in a bed that size? He couldn't remember.

"Good night, then," she said. "I'm having a long bath and curling up with a book. See you tomorrow morning. I usually leave here at eight thirty. Coffee drinkers will be waiting for the doors to open."

He nodded again, his heart falling out of his chest and landing on hot pink carpet right beside a polka-dotted, fake leather bean bag covered with stuffed animals of all sizes and sorts. Not that he minded being ready to go to work at that hour. No sir, he'd be glad to get out of a room that looked like it had been sprayed down with Pepto-Bismol. The only positive thing about the room he'd agreed to rent for fifty dollars a week was the small television in the corner. At least he could watch the ten o'clock news if he hurried with his shower. What had made him want to sit down and cry was the size of that twin bed. He hadn't slept in a bed that size since . . . well, in a very long time.

The water was hot and plentiful for which Sonny was

truly thankful. Wrapped in a towel about half the size he liked, he peeked out the door to make sure Cameo was indeed in her room with a book. Once in his pretty pink room, he pulled on a pair of black silk pajama bottoms, shoved a dozen dolls off the pink bedspread, and picked up the remote control. One push on the power button gave him a fuzzy screen. Changing the channels didn't produce anything more than that.

Most likely the cable had come undone. He slung his feet over the side of the bed and started across the room to fix it so he could see the news. Halfway there he stepped on a jack hiding in carpet pile. Holding up one aching foot and stifling a scream, he hopped around the room like a one legged ruptured duck who'd just finished off a bottle of Crown Royal. Until he set his other foot down soundly on the same jack. Then he sat down in the floor and bit his tongue to keep from using R-rated language in a little girl's frilly room.

When he could crawl to the television set, he found there was no cable. Just an electrical plug, a VCR, and a whole array of movies. No news, but he could take his pick of *Little Mermaid, Land Before Time, Beauty and the Beast*, or any one of twenty other movies.

What did you expect for fifty dollars a week? His conscience asked bluntly.

"More than *Little Mermaid*," he whispered tersely under his breath as he carefully picked his way through the jack infested carpet back to the bed. Digging around in the duffel bag, he found the journal he'd been given earlier that morning. Part of the deal was a full account with details, but he was only doing a day by day play of the simplest nature. No way was he going into the description of the room he was living in.

Day One: Job found. Short order fry cook for the Strawberry Moon cafe just south of Davis, Oklahoma. Room rented in the house with the cafe manager whose name is Cameo (now, isn't that the by product of a hippie mother and renegade father) Johnson. Minimum wage. Six days a week. Nine A.M. to nine P.M. Sunday's free. Room rent, fifty dollars per week. Cameo could well be the girl who will consent to marry me by the end of the month.

He pulled the comforter back to find Barbie sheets. Slipping between them, he laced his fingers behind his head, stared up at the ceiling, and hoped the month would go by fast.

On the opposite end of the house, Cameo prepared a bank deposit for the next morning and went through April's notes. April was Joyce's sister, the real owner of the Strawberry Moon. She'd carefully made notes for Joyce so she would have no trouble running the cafe while April, her husband, and two little girls spent a month in Mexico. When Joyce decided to go along with them and Cameo picked up the reins to run the cafe, she'd been mighty glad to have the notes. Tomorrow the produce delivery man came and the next day the delivery man for the frozen foods.

She heard the shower stop running and soft footsteps down the hall to Sonny's room. She dragged a chair over to the locked door of her bedroom and shoved the back under the door knob. He really didn't seem like the sort to murder her in her sleep for the vinyl bank bag she'd carried home, but a girl couldn't be too careful. As it was Joyce would probably drop graveyard dead if she knew what Cameo had done to get Sonny to work at the cafe. To think she'd brought a strange man into April's home would sure enough send her up in flames. One who was most likely really in the government witness protection program. But by golly, he could make an onion burger, and for the next month that's all that mattered!

"What she doesn't know won't hurt her," Cameo said softly as she turned on the water in the tub. "I just agreed to work at a minimum paying job for a month. We didn't go into details about how I planned to keep my job and not lose the bet. It's not like I'm going to marry the man."

Chapter Two

Cameo awoke to the smell of coffee drifting under her burglar proof door. Surely Sonny wasn't up already. The sun had barely chased away the darkness of the night. She tugged the pale blue, satin designer nightshirt over her head and tossed it on the bed, found a pair of clean jogging shorts and a tee shirt in her suitcase, and was running her fingers through her tangled curly hair as she followed her nose to the kitchen.

"You're an early riser," she said.

"Yes, I am. The early bird gets the worm and all. Coffee is ready. I didn't need training to make a mean cup of strong coffee," he said, sipping a cup of steaming black coffee and reading the morning paper someone had thrown at the door. Actually that's what had awakened him half an hour before—the sound of the newspaper hitting the metal storm door.

"Not interested in the worm, but I will have a cup of coffee," she said, inhaling the warm fumes from the coffee before actually indulging in the first hot gulp. "I do an early morning run before I open the cafe," she said, explaining the shorts and tee shirt when she felt his stare over the top of the newspaper.

"Me too. Where do we run? Down the highway? Or is there a gym in Davis?" He asked.

"There's a privately owned gym, I'm told, but with the hours I put in I don't have time for it. It closes at ten o'clock in the evening and there's no way I can get the cafe cleaned up and get there before closing. And by then I'm too tired to do a workout anyway. The gates to the football field are open all the time and there's a track around it, so that's where I run every morning. Not in the best of shape, but it's a track. I run for thirty minutes," she said.

"I'm ready soon as I get my shoes on," he told her.

Lovely, she thought. *Now I work with you all day, live in the same house with you at night, and you run with me in the mornings. All with someone I really do not like, but if I want a cook, I suppose I have to be nice. At least you don't have a forked tail and a pitchfork, though, so for that I shall be grateful. And you don't have any idea I've got a bank account so you won't be sweet talking me for that.*

"Give me ten minutes," she said coolly. "I don't jog. I run. But you can walk if you aren't up to a thirty minute run."

"I reckon I can keep up," he noted the ice in her voice. "Want to ride on the back of the cycle? I don't have an extra helmet but if you're willing to risk it, you're welcome."

She thought about that for a moment, hesitating to

consider the risk. Good grief, it was only a mile all the way into town and the football field was closer than that if they turned down Atlanta Street and went in that way. Riding with him would be better than offering to let him ride in the car. He couldn't jerk a gun from under his shirt, take her to a remote area, and kill her for the Lexus—not if she was on the back of his cycle.

"Sure, why not?" She finally said.

He didn't even look up, hiding his big grin behind the newspaper.

An hour later he leaned over at the waist, hands on his shaky thighs, and panted at the south end of the Davis Wolves football field. That wiry woman surely did mean it when she said she was going to run, not jog. In thirty minutes they'd all-out run four miles; sixteen times around the track. He knew exactly because keeping track of the laps and trying to keep up with her was all he could do. Any other thoughts were pushed aside.

"Winded?" She asked.

"Very," he admitted. "Why do you run like that?"

"Because it's good for me. Clears the cob webs out of my brain and gives me a fresh slate for the rest of the day," she fell down on the green grass on the field and shut her eyes against the glaring sun. It was going to be another hot one, but then a person with two healthy brain cells to rub together didn't expect anything else in Texas or Oklahoma in June.

"You do this every day?"

"Here, I do. When I'm at the . . . depends on where I am. I like a treadmill in the dead of winter," she said.

"What did you start to say? When you are where?" He asked.

"No past. No future, Sonny," she reminded him, sitting up and drawing her knees up under her chin. "Either you show me some of yours or you don't get any of mine."

"Then I guess it doesn't matter where that treadmill is. Must be seven o'clock by now. You ready for breakfast?" He asked. *The treadmill is probably one of those non-motorized ones on the back porch of a house somewhere back in the sticks*, he thought. *She might run like she's an athlete and put on airs like she's the daughter of a sheik, but that's all it is, just airs. But at least she's a waitress and that's fine and dandy. Just exactly what I need while I'm confined to the borders of Murray County, Oklahoma, showing two old codgers that I can live, work, and love all on minimum wage. At least she won't be thinking of my bank account when she says she'll marry me.*

"I have yogurt and fresh fruit at the house. I usually eat a salad for dinner at the cafe and then have something from the menu for supper. You want anything else we'll have to go to the grocery store before we go back," she said.

"I usually make a fruit smoothie with plain yogurt and fruit. Is there a blender at the house?" He asked.

That sure didn't sound like prison fare to Cameo. If he was in the WP program it was probably for some white collar moneyed crime. Now that she'd had time to think about it, there was no way he was used to dressing in jeans and a tee shirt. He was the preppie type. Three pieced suits from Armani. Pinstriped shirts and conservative ties. He drove a Porsche and carried an eel briefcase in his real life. She was a whiz at judging people. That's how she got to be what she was in the Dallas

Oil Corporation. True, her grandfather started the company during the big Texas oil boom in the early 20's, and her father kept the business going strong even in the lean years, and someday the whole enchilada would belong to Cameo, or at least half of it now that they'd merged with Houston Enterprises, but she hadn't relied on her family to climb the ladder. No, sir, she'd done that on her own. Hours and hours of work and learning the business. In a month she'd be in the swankiest offices and living in the poshest penthouse in Austin, serving the new company, DH Oil Corporation, as one of the vice presidents. The one in charge of all the accounts and money end of the deals. The other one, a Will Dalhart, would take care of the drilling aspects. Her father had praised Will so much that she dreaded meeting the man. He was probably egotistical, bald, and demanding.

Besides, her father had wedding bells ringing in his ears every time he looked at the other VP. She could feel it. Just because she'd jumped that hurdle called thirty didn't mean her picture was hanging in the old maid's hall of fame. Come to think of it, Red had wedding bells ringing in his ears every time he looked at anyone wearing pants. He'd begun to carry on about not living long enough to even lay his eyes upon a grandchild. From the way he talked, a person would think Cameo would never produce an heir to Red Marshall's oil kingdom.

Why was it that everyone but Cameo thought her biological clock was about to explode? Lots of women had a family when they were older than thirty these days. It was the twenty first century, not the days of horses and buggies. Of course those women were a durn sight luckier in love than Cameo.

"Earth to Cameo, where are you?" Sonny waved a hand in front of her nose. "Is the grocery store open this early?"

"Opens at seven every morning," she said, leaving the future behind and letting herself be jerked back into reality.

"Then let's go buy more yogurt and fruit," he said. "We've got a long shift ahead of us. What time does your other waitresses come in?"

"You're lookin' at it, Sonny. You're the cook. I'm the waitress slash manager slash accountant," she told him. "How are we going to get food home on a motor cycle?"

"I got a small trunk under where you sit," he reminded her. "Just don't go buying gallons of milk or liters of Coke."

They crossed the railroad tracks and made a sharp left turn on First Street, passed a railroad-station-turned-museum on the left, and whipped a right onto Main Street. He spotted a barber shop, a car wash, a kid's clothing store, a Mexican restaurant, a drug store, three or four antique stores, and a two story building under construction across from the only red light in town, which was red and seemed like would never change. Davis, Oklahoma looked prosperous enough for a small town. At least there were few, if any, empty store buildings on the Main Street. Several little towns in Texas weren't so fortunate. They were in the last throes of death with one foot already in the grave called ghost town, the other on a banana peel named progress. With the decorated lamp poles and park benches placed between the stores, along with nice clean streets and store fronts, it looked like Davis might still be alive and kicking for many more years.

He saw the Sooner Food Store marquee even before she pointed in that direction. Bananas, chuck roast, and brisket were on sale. There were only half a dozen vehicles in the parking lot, four of them pickup trucks, so Sonny nosed his cycle into the place closest to the front door. Cameo was off the back and headed into the store so fast that he had to rush to catch up with her.

"Hey, Cameo, how's business?" One of the checkers yelled from the first cash register. "You run out of produce?"

"Not so far," Cameo said. "Looks like it's going to be a lovely day."

"Sure does. Who are you runnin' with?"

"I'm Sonny Johnson," he introduced himself.

"Well, I'll be danged. You didn't tell us you was married when you and Joyce come in here," the lady said.

"Guess she's ashamed of me," Sonny gave the checker his best grin, laying on the charm so thick it almost gagged Cameo.

"Oh, honey, I doubt that. A woman would be crazy to be ashamed of something pretty as you," the lady chuckled.

Sonny slipped his arm around Cameo's waist, playing the part of instant dutiful husband. "Well, Mrs. Johnson, what shall we buy?" He whispered seductively into her ear.

"Hush!" She snapped at him. The touch of his fingers sliding across her bare arm when he reached around her to pick up several bananas caused a warm spot in the middle of her stomach. Great heavens, she couldn't be affected by a man whose name was Sonny, had a tattoo, and rode a motorcycle. There'd been a string of men a mile long in the past eight years who had husband written in indelible ink across their fore-heads and she'd turned them all down because they didn't make her heart quiver. She'd at least have that much for his name on her checking account. Now out of the clear blue skies a stranger causes a flutter in her stomach and just look who and what he was!

Sonny added a mango, two kiwis, and a few oranges to the cart she pushed and asked about a fresh coconut, but she shook her head, taking him instead to the aisle where he could purchase a bag of coarsely ground coconut.

"Now why did you do that?" She hissed when she was certain they were alone.

"What?" He asked, raising an eyebrow in mock surprise.

"Let that lady think we were married." She said icily.

"We're not?" He asked.

"Oh, buy your coconut and let's get out of here," she whispered. "I'll deal with you later."

"Going to fire me?" He raised an eyebrow over twin-kling blue eyes.

"No, but I might make your life miserable," she taunted, pushing the cart up to the checker's stand.

"You helping at the Strawberry Moon?" the checker asked.

"Yes, ma'am. I'm the chief cook and bottle washer," he said.

"Well, I just think it's wonderful that ya'll are help-ing Joyce and April out so they can go down to Mexico on that mission. I been down there three years and it's sure enough a long, hot, hard job, but a good feeling one. That'll be eight dollars and sixty two cents," she said.

"We wouldn't have it any other way," Sonny said.

"Ya'll been out to Turner Falls yet, or over to Sulphur Park? Wonderful places for picnics. I know you only got Sunday off. April fusses about that part of the business, but she always uses Sunday after church to do something with the family. So next Sunday ya'll don't lay around being bored. Go on out and have a little adventure," she said. "By the way, the husband and I'll be stopping in at the Strawberry Moon for supper tonight. It's his night to cook and last time he tried his hand in the kitchen, I was afraid to even bury the casserole in the yard for fear I'd get hauled down to the jail for disposin' of hazardous waste material the wrong way. Besides, I just love those grilled onion burgers. You be nice to this husband of yours, Cameo. I think he's a keeper."

Cameo nodded and forced a smile. Sonny wasn't going to have to worry about some mob boss finding him and executing him with a single bullet at the nape of his neck. She'd do it for free, enjoy pulling the trigger, and even dig the hole under the wisteria bush in the backyard to bury his sorry carcass.

She seethed through breakfast, pretending he wasn't even in the same kitchen with her. They walked to work together but she was careful to keep her distance. Her nerves were jumbled enough without his hand brushing hers. She convinced herself that whole warm, fuzzy feeling was simply a ninety eight point six degree hand touching her arm, chilled by the air conditioning in the grocery store.

At least until they arrived at the back door of the cafe where she produced a key from the pocket of her tight fitting jeans and opened the door. When he reached to turn the knob his finger tips feathered across hers in a soft caress. Heat rose up from the pits of her insides to flush her face in high color. Good grief, what on earth was happening to her in this place? She'd definitely have to take a closer look at the "husband list" when she got to Austin next month.

Morning coffee drinkers kept her hopping until eleven o'clock and then there was the thirty minute lull before the noon rush. Sonny had everything in the kitchen arranged and ready. Potatoes were peeled, run through the fry cutter, and waiting in a five gallon bucket of water treated with some kind of white powder to keep them from getting dark. He'd asked the cook why they didn't just buy frozen potatoes and she'd informed him that April didn't believe in serving such fare. Meat patties were ready to throw on the grill. Nothing left to do, so he wandered up to the front, past the cash register and out into the dining area. Six booths and four tables each surrounded by six chairs awaited the lunch crowd. Forty eight people could be seated comfortably. That could mean that many orders at once. He frowned, his eyebrows becoming a solid shelf across his forehead. Talk about pressure. He could be under it in a hurry.

"So you ready?" She asked, sipping a tall glass of iced tea.

"Does the cook get to sit down if he's caught up?" Sonny asked.

"Sure. We have about thirty minutes before the noon rush hits. Grab a glass of tea or whatever you want to drink and come tell me all about what crime you're covering up in the witness protection program," she teased.

He filled a glass with crushed ice and water and joined her at the table she'd chosen. At first glance he'd thought Cameo was plain, kind of like . . . he frowned as he tried to remember the actresses name in that chick flick Felicia loved. *Steel Magnolias* was the name of the film. The woman was the plain looking beauty operator with glasses. Darryl Hannah, that's it. He smiled at his acute memory. It'd been at least a decade since he'd watched that movie. One time was enough with Felicia using a whole box of tissues.

Cameo was like Darryl Hannah, only shorter, and a bit thinner. But quite a lovely young lady, even with the thick glasses she wore. She had a thin, aristocratic nose probably from an English heritage gone bad some-where along the line, perhaps from a renegade father or mother who didn't give a hoot about their background. But the nose didn't lie—there was blue blood some-where in her background. Cameo had nice green eyes behind those thick lenses and strawberry blond hair, a bit too curly for his tastes but he wouldn't complain. After all, the whole situation had fallen out of heaven tied in a neat bow and perfect for what he needed this next month. He'd never believed in luck or coincidence either, but it had sure enough just happened, and Sonny wasn't about to kick it in the teeth.

"So how can you work as a waitress and drive a Lexus?" He asked. "Are you in the witness protection program too?"

She laughed. A clear, tinkling sound that lifted his heart right out of his chest. An honest laugh from a woman. He hadn't heard that in many, many years. Most of the women he was in contact with were so fake they didn't know how to laugh.

"You think that Lexus belongs to me? Honey, I don't drive a Lexus. That's my friend's car. Her name is Joyce. She's April's sister. April and her family own this business and the house we're living in. April's husband is a school teacher at Davis High School and the youth director at one of the churches in town. They all go to Mexico and build something in the summers. A mission thing. Anyway, Joyce wanted to go but she'd promised April she'd spend her four week vacation running the cafe. I offered to do the job while they were gone. The car is Joyce's but I've got the use of it to run into town for groceries or whatever," Cameo explained.

"I see," he said. That furthered his impression of the treadmill on the back porch of the run down house.

"And do you work for Joyce when you aren't working here? Or are you maybe a hair dresser?" He asked slyly.

"That's getting pretty close to asking questions which you have no right to ask. Which reminds me, if I'm going to pay you with a check, I need you to fill out tax forms," she said.

"Well, bring them on," he said. "I told you I've got a permanent address you can send the W2's."

Picking up her empty glass, she made her way to the counter and rustled around in a shoe box on the bottom shelf where the extra candy bars were stored. She found a faded form, tucked it under her arm, refilled her glass, and went back to the table. She produced a pen from the pocket of her tee shirt and handed both to him.

He carefully filled in Sonny Johnson and his real social security number. The government didn't give a royal rat's hind end what name a person went under so long as it got its fair share of what that person made. He filled in the post office box number he used for his personal business in Houston, Texas, and signed the strange name on the line where his signature was required. In a month, he'd be gone from Murray County, Oklahoma and no one would ever find him with nothing more than a box number to use for a clue.

"Thank you," she said. At least winning the wager she'd made with Joyce wasn't going to cost her over a thousand dollars. She could pay Sonny out of the cafe check book. "Here comes work," she nodded toward two pickup trucks parking out front.

"Then let's get to it," he grinned.

They kept a steady pace all day. Two van loads of Baptist church kids and their sponsors on their way to Falls Creek Baptist Church camp up in the Arbuckle Mountains kept them hopping even during the time when they were usually slow. By the time they mopped the floor and locked the doors, they were both ready for showers and bed. Sonny went his way down the hall and she dragged her tired body through her own borrowed bedroom door, forgetting even to set the chair under the door knob before she sunk into the tub and then went to bed.

Staring at the ceiling, she wondered if she'd make it through the whole month. She had to, simply had to, to prove the point. Letting her mind drift back to the argument she'd had with Joyce, her secretary and best friend, and her cagey old father, she laced her fingers behind her head and played out the scene again. It was by far the stupidest wager she'd ever let herself be goaded into.

Cameo shook the wager from her head and beat her pillow into a soft place to lay her head. A week hadn't even gone by and even in her bone tired, worn out state she missed the lights of the big city. The people in Davis were friendly enough. Kind. Accepting. Nothing she could complain about, but it wasn't home. She even missed the hard mental work of keeping an oil corporation running. All she had to look forward to were days and days with only Sonny. A witness protection ex-con willing to work for minimum wage who drank smoothies for breakfast. She sighed and fell asleep, dreaming of making one of yogurt, strawberries, bananas, and a cup full of arsenic and smiling while Sonny Johnson drank every drop. She watched him drop dead at her toes, then with a smile accepted a brief case full of diamonds from a man who looked like Marlon Brando. Not bad pay for her first assassination.

Down the hall, Sonny put the *Beauty and the Beast* movie in the VCR. That should bore him to sleep in five minutes. He picked up the journal and carefully wrote: *Today was my first full day of work. Tired but determined. Under those hideous black framed glasses, Cameo Johnson is really a lovely young woman. She has no idea who or what I am and since she's the only woman I have contact with, she may be the one who will say she'll marry me . . .*

That was enough for today. He hadn't promised to give even that many details. Just that he'd keep a loose journal while he was away so they'd know how he spent his days and if he succeeded in his mission. He fell asleep long before the end of the movie.

Chapter Three

Cameo shivered when she eased her feet into the water at what the local folks called Little Niagara on the backside of the Chickasaw National Recreation Area. It was actually just a public park covering acres and acres, with a creek rambling through it—a lovely place, there under the shade trees for a Sunday afternoon picnic. Sonny had gone off on a hike to a place the people in the nature center called Bromide Hill. She'd read a big thick romance book for a while then laid it aside to watch a group of children diving from the top of the small waterfall.

Not once in her life had she ever been swimming in anything other than a heated indoor pool, but something about the youngsters' giggles and freedom called out to her. If she didn't think about minnows or even bigger fish occupying that water, or the fact there wasn't a drop of chlorine tossed in to purify the water, she might even like a swim in the natural elements.

At least that's what she told herself bravely until she stepped out on the top step and the icy water made her toes try to crawl back inside her foot. Goose bumps the size of fresh coconuts broke out all over her slim body. She swore if her bikini hadn't already been blue it would have been by the time she retraced her two foot-steps back to the safety of the sandbar.

"Hey, Momma's here," a high pitched little boy's voice said behind her.

Two warm hands landed on her bare back and pushed. One minute she was balanced precariously on one foot trying to get out of the cold water without actually setting her foot down into it. The next she flew through the hot breeze like a leaf and hit the frigid water with a splash. The shock froze her brain as well as her body. She went down until her feet hit bottom. She opened her eyes and clawed her way back toward the top. At one point her hand brushed against a slip-pery, slimy object and she hoped sincerely that it was a fish and not a snake. She broke the surface in a rush, gasping for air, and shivering, swearing that her first assassination wouldn't be Sonny after all. She'd receive her lethal injection for strangling two snaggle-toothed kids.

"That ain't Momma," one little boy yelled at his broth-er. "You done throwed in the wrong Momma, Josh."

"Huh-oh," Josh blinked twice and looked down from the top of the short little dam. "I'm sorry, ma'am."

She had a speech on the tip of her tongue that would boil the water she was dog paddling in, but the look on those two kids' faces took the meanness right out of her. Even without her glasses, their little faces looked

Carolyn Brown

so pitiful she almost laughed. That and the sight of Sonny meandering back to their blanket. At least she hoped it was Sonny. It looked like the way he walked and he was sitting on their blanket where her glasses had been left beside her book. Hopefully he wouldn't sit on them. She'd only brought one pair with her. Heaven help her if they were broken.

"Shhhh," she placed a finger over her mouth and nodded toward Sonny. "Don't say a word about the water being cold."

"Yes, ma'am," Josh grinned. "Want me to push him in too?"

"That would be wonderful," Cameo grinned at the two impish little boys, evidently twins, one with his two upper teeth missing. The other with his two lower ones gone, leaving a gap in a wide grin. Her body had begun to adjust to the cold water and it actually felt good. She wondered if she'd ever sweat again, though. It would take a lifetime for her body to reach a normal ninety eight point six.

"How's the water?" Sonny asked, working hard to keep from snarling his nose. He'd heard that people swam in creek water before but he'd never been in a position to actually see it. Now the ocean was a different matter. He loved the beaches in France, the ones in Florida, even the ones near his home town of Galveston. But a narrow little creek with screaming children was a different matter all together. No telling what kind of garbage was at the bottom. Dead fish. Snakes. Rotted food from where kids fed the fish.

"Oh, it's fine," Cameo said, paddling around like she really enjoyed it, when in reality she was afraid to let her feet touch the bottom again. There was still mud squished up between her toes from when she kicked off the bottom in an effort to reach the top. At least she hoped it was mud. It felt like slimy, rotted lettuce that had been left in the 'fridge for a month or two.

"You swim here often?" He came closer and squatted near the edge of the water.

"No, first time I've ever been in this park," she answered honestly. "Come on in. It'll cool you off from your hike."

"No thanks," he shook his head.

"Too good for the likes of creek water?" She taunted.

"I don't swim in anything that I can't see the bottom of. And I prefer a filter with a good purifying apparatus," he said.

"Must've been a good life before you got caught at whatever sin you committed," she grinned, her eyes twinkling with mischief.

"No past," he reminded her. "But rest assured the sin I committed doesn't warrant me getting wet in that. Neither does any amount of sweat. I'll just stay stinky until we get back to the trailer and then I'll take a shower."

"We don't think so," the two little boys rushed from behind him, placed their hands on his bare back and, with a mighty shove, sent him cannon balling into the cold water.

Sonny barely had time to fill his lungs before the frosty water engulfed him. His first thought was that somewhere upstream there was an iceberg the creek ran across before flowing through the park. He'd never been so cold in his whole life, not even on Swiss ski slopes. His head hit the murky bottom first but it didn't take him but a moment to get himself turned around and shoot toward the top. The first thing he saw when he broke the surface was Cameo laughing so hard tears rolled down her cheeks.

"You told them to do that," he sputtered, swimming toward the edge until he could get a foot hold on the slippery bottom. It would take all the hot water in the trailer to get him clean when they got home, but he wasn't going to feel one bit guilty about using it. Yuck, yuck. What was that between his toes? He wondered as he climbed back up on the bank.

"Yes, I did," she said, following him.

"Why? Don't I work hard for you, woman? Why would you try to kill me?" He asked as he pulled himself up near the grassy bank.

"Help me," she held out a hand.

Without thinking he reached for her hand, only to have her flip backwards, taking him back into the water with her. Sure, she hadn't ever been swimming in these waters before. That was a blatant lie if Sonny ever heard one. She was a creek swimmer like the rest of these people and she'd duped him. Most likely knew those two little snaggle-toothed boys laughing so hard at the stunt they'd pulled. They were probably her nephews.

He came up the second time right next to her. When he had a solid footing, he reached down and picked her up like a new bride and waded out onto the bank with her still held close to his chest. She fit well in his arms and for a minute he forgot she was just a waitress. He couldn't remember the last time he'd had so much simple fun.

No strings attached.

No underlying currents.

No wondering if the woman of the day was simply after his money or if she really liked him.

"That was evil," he shook drops of water from his hair like a wet hound dog.

"Hey, you're getting it on my book," she snatched her novel away and tucked it in a fold of the blanket.

"Why do you read such trivial nonsense?" He asked.

"Because I like it," she said. "And I'm not evil. You got to admit, it cooled you off after that hike."

"Cooled me off. It would take a trek through the Sahara to warm my blood up again," he flopped back on the pallet, shielded his eyes with the back of his hand and pretended to fall asleep.

Emotions ripped through Cameo's heart leaving dozens of questions in their wake. Her skin stung from the touch of his hands, hot meeting cold in a battle. She couldn't let herself fall for Sonny. Not even if he was just kidding about the witness protection program. He was a drifter; said so himself. He'd only promised her a month at the Strawberry Moon and then he'd be gone on that big motorcycle and she'd never see him again. He'd vowed there would be no answers to any questions about his past and that's how lasting relationships were born—in a medley of the past, present, and future blending together to make one moment, one heart, one soul.

True, they'd worked fantastically well together all week. One fourth of the time had passed quickly with him in the kitchen and her up front. They shared the clean-up every night and went home to their own rooms. The past two nights she'd even forgotten to lock the bedroom door. She was more comfortable with Sonny Johnson than she'd ever been with another human being in her life. Not even Joyce came close in the running and they'd been friends for years.

It must be the fact that she wasn't Ivy Marshall in Davis, Oklahoma. She was Cameo Johnson, the waitress who ran the Strawberry Moon. The lady who laughed with the clerks at the grocery store, who served up onion burgers to the regular customers, and who even joked with Sonny the night he burned six hamburgers and had to start all over again.

She stretched out on her stomach, careful not to let her leg touch Sonny's. She didn't need the feelings he evoked in her heart. Not now. Not ever. She'd go to war to keep from falling for a drifter with no future or past. Even if the war meant a broken heart later down the line when no other man made her heart skip a beat when he looked up from a grill full of onions and hamburger patties and smiled brightly at her. What couldn't be simply could not be. Ivy Cameo Marshall-Johnson was a grown woman and she'd nip this little physical attraction right in the bud.

"Hey, what're you two doing here?" A lady asked.

Cameo's eyes snapped open and looked up at a regular in the cafe, but she couldn't remember the woman's name. "A little relaxation after a long grueling week at the Moon," she said, trying desperately to drag the name from the dusty attic of her brain.

"I don't know if you'll remember me," the woman sat down uninvited on the edge of the blanket. "I'm Christy Smith. Come into your place once a week or so. Work down at the Falls in the office. Anyway, my husband and I are involved with the same church as April and her family. We sure miss them when they go on the mission work every summer. I'd like to invite you two to our young married group tonight. It's a social pot-luck dinner. You don't have to bring a thing but your-selves and an appetite. We all think it's pretty nice what you're doing for April."

Cameo had her mouth open to refuse the invitation. She didn't want to get close to any of the local people. Do her penance and go on home to her own way of life, was the way she had it figured out. Home to a big Caddy, maybe a red one with lots of gold trim, and every option the company had to offer. Her father would rue the day he'd made a wager with his daughter, by golly.

"We'd love to," Sonny said. "What time do I bring this healthy appetite and where is the church?"

"Right off Main Street," Christy grinned. "Be a good way for you to get to know the other young married folks. Most of us haven't been married more than a year or two. Got a couple that will be moving up to the young parent's group in a few months. By the way, how long have you two been married?"

"Few months," Sonny reached across the pallet and clamped his hand around Cameo's. "Sure we can't bring something?"

"I'm sure," Christy said. "There'll be enough casseroles and food to feed the homeless in New York City on Christmas Day. I'll get on. I'm supposed to meet my husband, Richard, in the nature center in ten min-utes. Saw you all here, though, and wanted to invite you."

"Thank you," Cameo said weakly.

"Now why did you do that?" She jerked her burning hand free and slapped Sonny on the arm right above his tattoo. "I wasn't going to get all chummy with the local people."

Sonny snapped his head around to stare at her. "And why? I thought you were one of the locals. You telling me you're not from around these parts? Way you took to that yucky water, I figured you for a local, yourself."

"No past," she reminded him, poking his bare, sexy, hairy chest with her finger. "Why do you want to go mingle amongst the young married couples?"

"Why, darlin', to eat good casseroles," he laughed.

Chapter Four

What on earth did one wear to a church social in Davis, Oklahoma? Cameo had brought only one dress with her, not expecting to do a bit of socializing. A towel twirled turban style around her head and another wrapped around her slim body, she tapped a wet foot in front of the closet. Six pair of jeans, six tee shirts, one dress. That narrowed it down tremendously. The spaghetti strapped sundress and matching sandals would have to do, and if Sonny got a wild hair in the BVD's she'd seen hanging lopsided on the line at morning before they went on their picnic, then he could just scratch and deal with it. He probably didn't know, anymore than she did, what to wear to such an affair. Give her a business meeting with the oil sheiks of the world and she'd pull out a silk suit, three inch heels, and gold jewelry. A cocktail party with Dallas's young singles, and she'd wear a simple emerald green dress with diamonds hanging from her ears and around her neck. But part of the deal was that she'd leave behind her wardrobe and bring only work clothes, plus one dress and pair of shoes, if they were fairly simple, just in case. She turned this way and that, eyeing her reflection in the floor length mirror attached to the back of the sliding closet doors. Since she had no other choice it would have to do. She'd look much better without the glasses, but that was a genetic problem passed down by her deceased mother. As soon as the minor infection cleared up, she'd be back in her contact lenses—hopefully by the time she finished her stint at the cafe and stepped into the conference room at the new oil business in Austin.

Sonny raised an eyebrow in appreciation when she opened the door to her bedroom on the other end of the trailer from his pink and white princess kingdom. Her hair was twisted up with a wild array of curls on the top of her head. The cotton dress with straps no wider than his little finger fit her slim figure like it had been tailor made for her, and he'd be willing to bet dollars to onion burgers those were Italian leather sandals on her feet. She'd probably borrowed the whole get-up from her friend, Joyce, the one who owned the Lexus out there under the carport. If it weren't for those glasses perched on her nose, she'd be a right good looking woman.

"Ready?" He asked.

"How many church socials have you attended?" She asked.

He frowned, his blue eyes brooding under a ledge of heavy brows. "Afraid this is a first for me. You've been to a bunch of church socials I'd bet."

"What I do about church isn't up for grabs either,

Sonny. But to answer your question, this is a first for me too," she said.

"Then look out world. Here comes the ex-con and the waitress to your social," he opened the door for her.

Christy greeted them at the door of the fellowship hall and escorted them into the huge room. An eight-foot fold-up table covered with a white table cloth displayed enough casseroles that Sonny might not be hungry for days. A matching table set at right angles to the first one offered a menagerie of desserts. By tomorrow Cameo's only dress would be two sizes too small if she sampled everything that looked good.

"Hey, everyone, this is Sonny and Cameo Johnson. They're the ones helping April out with the Strawberry Moon this month. Come around and make yourselves known to them. Now if Brad will say grace we'll get started with supper," Christy raised her voice enough to get everyone's attention.

"And you can sit by me and the other ladies," she whispered the moment Brad said, "Amen."

"Okay," Cameo nodded.

"Load your plates, now," Christy said. "If anyone goes home hungry it's your own fault. Silver and napkins are on the table. So all you have to balance is your plate and drink."

Cameo slid a wedge of spinach quiche onto her paper plate and dipped into a lovely green salad. Maybe these socials weren't such a bad idea after all. She'd lived on a light breakfast, lettuce and tomato salad lunch, and an onion burger supper all week. Real food looked good.

Christy motioned her to a place beside her and at least ten other women at a big round table. Cameo had barely set her plate and plastic cup of sweet iced tea on the table when Christy began telling her the names of everyone at the table.

"Now you know everyone's names, even though you won't possibly remember them all," Christy laughed, "and we want to know the scoop."

Oh yes, I'll remember them, Cameo thought. *This lady doesn't realize part of my job is remembering not only a person's name but what they like to drink, who their wife is, and how many kids they have.*

"Scoop?" Cameo filled her mouth with quiche. Lord Almighty, it was wonderful. Whoever made it could come and live in the penthouse in Austin and she'd pay her handsomely just to cook three meals a day.

"Yes, where did you and that handsome hunk come from and are you really Joyce's secretary?" Christy asked.

Every ear was turned to her, waiting to hear the scoop.

"Who made this lovely quiche?" Cameo tried to sidestep the issue.

"Millie did. She's the one over there at the table where your husband is sitting. The bottle blond with big boobs who's eyeing Sonny like she could have him for breakfast," Christy said. "Now that she's seen him, I'm sure she'll take on a fancy for onion burgers these next three weeks."

"Good grief, I thought this was a young married Christian group," Cameo said.

"It is. But just because we're young and married and Christian don't make us saints," Christy said.

"Sure don't make Millie one," Twyla, the mousey brunette with big brown eyes said. "But she can make a good quiche. Not that Christy ain't right, though. She'll be down at the Strawberry Moon trying to yank Sonny right out from under your covers soon as the doors open tomorrow morning."

"So you want to know the scoop?" Cameo whispered. "Well, here it is. The ladies down at the Sooner Food store made a big mistake. I'm Cameo Johnson and Johnson is one of the most common names in the whole world. Anyway, Sonny's last name is Johnson too. But we're not married."

"Oh, my Lord," Jane pressed her palm against her chest. "You mean you're living with him . . . in sin?"

"Oh don't go having a cardiac arrest on us right here in the middle of supper, Jane. You might have given up all your vices but it don't mean the rest of us are as saintly as you are," Christy said. "Tell us more," she nodded toward Cameo.

"Well, I do work with Joyce. She's my best friend as well," Cameo said.

"I knew it. April told me that Joyce's cohort was going to run the cafe so Joyce could go with them on the mission. She was all excited because there's a bachelor man from right here in Davis going, too, and she was going to try to fix him up with Joyce. Just so you know, he's a nice man. Got his own business and all," Twyla said.

"That's not what I was talking about. Tell us more about Sonny and you," Christy said.

"I came to work in the cafe for Joyce while she's gone to Mexico," Cameo said between bites. "April put an ad in the paper for a cook and said there would be lots of applicants. But there wasn't a single one."

"April didn't run an ad," Jane said, tilting her head defiantly. "I read *The Davis News* from front to back every week and there wasn't an ad. I was hoping she would need a cook because my younger sister needs a summer job. She just graduated from high school and will be off to college this fall. Then when I heard it was a husband and wife team, I understood."

"But Joyce said it had already run and it would . . ." Cameo stammered. She would wring Joyce's neck when she returned. That wench wasn't about to let her win the bet. There had never been an ad and without a cook, Cameo would have no choice but to back out of the wager.

"So there wasn't an ad," Christy threw up her hands in despair. "How did you talk Sonny into cooking for you? You were already living together in Texas right?"

"No, I'd never seen him before. He rode up to the Strawberry Moon on his motorcycle and I asked him if he was looking for a job. He said he was so I hired him on the spot. The cook trained him and then she left. He said he needed a place to live and only a month's worth of work, so I rented him one of the bedrooms in the trailer. We're only there to sleep anyway, since we're at the cafe from nine to nine," Cameo said.

"You just hired a man right off the street?" Jane almost hyperventilated.

"How romantic," Twyla sighed. "And to think he's that handsome to boot. Lord, girl, you'd better keep him on a short leash though or Millie is going to slip him right out from under you."

"But she's really married," Cameo stammered.

"Yes, she is. Feller sitting right there on the end. The one with the bald spot on the back of his head and the gold rimmed glasses. He's her parents' choice of husband. She fell head over heels in love with a poor old boy in high school. Too handsome for words. But come from a poor family and her parents pitched one great big hissy fit. Said they hadn't raised her and spent all that money for her to marry some redneck deer hunter. Sent her back east to college. Billy Tom was pretty tore up for a while but then he joined the Marines. Last any of us heard he was doing right well. Been everywhere in the world but back here to Davis. Millie came home at Christmas, wilder than ever and flunked out of school. The next year her old daddy hired Frank to manage his business and they pushed the marriage right through the church. Millie's just got a wild itch Frank ain't able to scratch. Biggest flirt in town," Christy said.

"And she'll flirt Sonny right out of your arms," Twyla said.

"But I'm not married to him," Cameo said.

"But if you wanted to brand him, you'd hate to have the memory of him snuggled up to Millie in the front seat of her big old Lincoln Town Car out on a back country road, now wouldn't you?" Christy said. "So tell us about Sonny? Who is he? Where's he from?"

"Have no idea. He's a pretty good cook. Only burned a few burgers and the stray cat at April's doesn't seem to mind too bad when he does that. He wears BVD's and hangs them up crooked so I don't think he's used to doing his own laundry. But then if he's an ex-con or really in the witness protection program he probably doesn't do laundry," Cameo laughed. So church socials weren't one nickel's worth of difference from cocktail parties. Iced tea instead of martinis. Paper plates full of casseroles instead of stuffed olives and caviar on a cracker. Plastic cups instead of fine crystal. Gossip was the same, though.

"Well, well, what are you all talking about over here?" Millie asked from five feet away as she approached the table. She carried a plate laden with small portions of at least ten desserts. Cameo looked at the paper plate and the thought chased through her mind that she'd give Sonny and his motorcycle in exchange for the plate.

"We were discussing this wonderful quiche," Cameo said glibly with a big smile. "Whoever made it should put it in a restaurant and cook for a living."

"Well, thank you," Millie fluffed her blond hair over her shoulder. "Any one of these hussies could have told you I made that quiche, and yes, I am a wonderful cook. Now tell me about you, Ms. Johnson. I understand you work with April's sister, Joyce. You her secretary or something? Mercy, I just can't see that handsome hunk over there married to a secretary like you, though."

"He's not," Cameo smiled.

Sonny followed some fellow back to the casserole table for a second plate of food. The only woman at their table had finally yawned and declared she was sick of listening to sports talk. She was poison, pure poison, or Sonny would eat his brand new sneakers for breakfast the next morning after he'd run in them. Sonny had seen her caliber dolled up in cocktail dresses, in business suits, in jeans and tee shirts. They were barracudas looking for a little minnow called a man to gobble up for supper. He pitied the quiet man at the end of the table whom she'd introduced with a touch of bitterness in her voice as her husband. Sonny had entertained notions that he could be wrong about the woman, right up to the time she reached under the table and squeezed his thigh just before she excused herself. Poison, pure poison.

"You'll have to watch out for Millie," Thatcher said as they both heaped Mexican casserole onto their plates.

"Oh?" Sonny played as dumb as he could.

"She's not been happy since high school. Wally, that'd be her husband, isn't the man she loved. She married him but she ain't loved him. She's always flirtin' around with any new pair of pants that comes riding into town. Wally, he just ignores it since he works for her daddy. I guess he figures it's part of his job to be blind where Millie is concerned."

"I see. Seen women like that before," Sonny nodded. "Think OU will have a good season this fall?"

"Oh, man, I hope so. Already got a bet riding on them in the first game. Me and Wally, we just do us some friendly betting. He never has liked OU. He's a graduate of OSU and man, you'd think he built the college," Thatcher laughed.

"No, I didn't build it," Wally said with a chuckle as he joined them. "But it's the best school in the state and next year they're going to prove it. Bet you a hundred dollars they stomp OU right into the ground."

"You're on," Thatcher said. "Tried any of this Mexican? It's pretty good. Twyla sure knows how to cook, don't she?"

"Yep, she does," Wally said wistfully.

"Hey, didn't mean to drag up old memories," Thatcher said, turning a bit red around the neck and ears.

"Sometimes it happens. Twyla and me were kind of seeing each other when Millie and me . . . oh, it's a long story not worthy of repeatin'," Wally said, bitterness in his voice.

"I understand," Sonny nodded. "Now you really think there's a chance OSU will whip OU next fall?"

"Chance? Man, it's going to happen. Sure as I'm standing here today, I'm going to take Thatcher's money and spend it on a brand new fishing rod," Wally smiled.

Church social, Sonny thought as he listened to the men around the table discussing sports, business, the price of stocks, and the wars in the third world countries. Church social. Cocktail party. One and the same. The only difference was the food was better at the church social. Men were the same, no matter if they came from a small town or a big city; if they were college graduates or ditch diggers. They liked the same thing. They loved with the same passion. They endured the same battles and disappointments.

Sonny wondered how Cameo was faring at her table full of women. He listened to the latest topic about the streets in Davis and the city council's opinion on the matter, and glanced over toward Cameo. Millie had pulled up a chair between Cameo and Christy and seemed to be doing most of the talking.

Church social. Didn't change much for the women either. The head she-coon of the Davis church social had just donned her crown and was holding court. He'd have to ask Cameo tomorrow what the woman had to say.

Chapter Five

"And what were you and those women talking about?" Sonny asked as they walked up on the porch.

"Same thing you men were," Cameo was glad it was dark and he couldn't see the high color filling her cheeks. Good Lord, she hadn't blushed like that since she was a teenager.

"The OU-OSU ball game?" He asked, merriment filling his voice as he waited for her to unlock the door to the trailer.

"Sure we were," she lied glibly. "What do you big strong men think we talk about? You? Do you talk about us every waking minute?"

"Sure we do," he lied with a chuckle.

The front door swung open and the telephone set up a ringing howl at the same time. *Saved by the bell*, Cameo thought, as she trotted to the bedroom. "That'll be Joyce reminding me that the produce man comes tomorrow," she threw over her shoulder as she shut the door and grabbed the receiver.

"Hello," she said quietly.

"Cameo, is that you? It sounds like you are in a tunnel," Joyce's high pitched voice came through so clear it was as if she were in the same room with Cameo.

"It's me," Cameo raised her voice an octave.

"That's better. I just got this strange call from Jane. Said you were at the young married social tonight," Joyce said.

"That's right," Cameo grinned. "I don't think it was in the rules of the game that I couldn't go to church was it?"

"With a husband? What have you done?" Joyce all but yelled.

"I'm thirty years old. I've run a pretty prosperous oil company for years and I think I know what I'm doing. I hired a cook. He needed a place to stay. He's paying April fifty dollars a week for a bedroom. He's only burned a few burgers so far and we're making a profit at the Strawberry Moon. It wasn't in the rules that you had to tell me the truth about the lack of an ad for a cook and it wasn't in the rules that I couldn't hire whomever I so desired. So I guess the wager is still on," Cameo said curtly.

Joyce laughed. "Jane says he's in the witness protection program. What kind of crime did he commit? Red would lay down and die if he knew you were living with a man of that caliber."

"I don't have my wardrobe which I'm missing sorely. I've had withdrawal symptoms from my cell phone. I'm living quite nicely on minimum wage. Daddy figured I'd lay down and die from any one of those three. Like I said, I'm thirty. I'm a pretty damn good judge of character and I'm not changing the arrangements unless you want to break the rules and come home? Then I'll gladly go to the south of France for the next three weeks."

"Don't you turn this around to be my fault. Keep your cook. If he robs April blind or kills you in your sleep just remember you asked for it all. What's his name anyway? Have you run him through the computer?"

"What computer? I don't think I'm allowed anything so modern. His name is Sonny Johnson and the ladies down at the grocery store thought we were married since we share the same last name. Of course mine isn't Johnson so we really don't. Anyway, that's the way the story got started. I put an end to it tonight, though. I told all those women that we weren't married," Cameo said.

"Oh. My. Lord."

"What now? I told the truth," Cameo asked.

"Now you're living with the cook who you hired off the street, who has a tattoo on his big sexy biceps, and who rides a motorcycle. April will never live it down. We may have to exorcise the Strawberry Moon," Joyce said.

"Did Jane say his biceps were sexy? If she used a word like sexy, she'll be praying all night," Cameo giggled.

"Oh, hush. The produce man comes on Monday. The list is in my notebook. You better keep that cook on a short leash and tired. I heard Millie was all over him," Joyce said.

"Millie can have him if he's got enough energy to do anything other than sleep after twelve hours in the kitchen at the cafe," Cameo's eyebrows knit together above her glasses. A jealous streak fired through her heart and battled the words as soon as they were shot through the phone lines to Mexico.

"So is that all you've got to report after a week in the cafe?" Joyce asked.

"That's all. I've got it under control. You'd best get ready to spend Christmas in Austin and Daddy better be talking to the Caddy dealer. I'm thinking a red one would be nice," Cameo said.

"I'll call you next week and we'll see then if you've got the same attitude," Joyce told her.

"Before you hang up, how are things in Mexico? I hear there's a young feller down there who's interested in robbing you of your heart," Cameo said.

"I might strangle April and shoot my brother-in-law for this stunt. The man is smothering me plumb to death. Nice oozes out of him. Can't even get a good argument going," Joyce said in desperation.

"Kissed you yet?"

"Hush. Did your cook kiss you yet?"

"I don't kiss and tell," Cameo laughed.

"Neither do I," Joyce said. "Yes, and it did not set off any bells or whistles. Matter of fact it was so gentle, it made me want to grab his ears and show him what a real kiss is supposed to be like. Now, I'm hanging up and you be careful. I should've known it wouldn't matter where you were, you'd stir up the whole place."

"Yes, ma'am, that's what I'm noted for. Graceless Plain Jane Creates Havoc," Cameo said. "Have a good week. Build a nice house, enjoy Mr. Nice, and be nice."

"Good-bye," Joyce said.

The sound of a loud click and then a soft dial tone filled Cameo's ears. She twirled around in the bedroom floor a dozen times and then did a deep bow. She'd won the first round and survived the first week. Ah, but victory was sweet.

The morning coffee drinkers lingered on until noon that Monday. Cameo dealt with the produce man for the second time, making him reimburse her for ten heads of sorry lettuce he'd pawned off on her the week before. She helped slice enough tomatoes to get them through the dinner and supper rush; peel twenty pounds of potatoes for French fries; thinly slice so many onions her eyes were watery and her hands smelly as she refilled coffee mugs. Not one of the elderly men seemed to notice. Maybe the coffee scorched their ability to smell as well as their tongues.

Right in the middle of the lunch rush she turned around to find Millie and Jane sliding into the only empty booth in the dining room. Now if that wasn't a combination. Maybe Millie brought Jane along like a rosary. When Millie sinned, Jane would pray her out of hell. Cameo swallowed the giggle that visual produced and patted the pocket of her stained apron to make sure she still had an order pad and pen.

"Help you ladies?" She asked.

"Yes," Millie said. "I want the grilled onion burger basket and the biggest Dr. Pepper you can make. About the time I get finished I want a thick chocolate malt with extra malt, and where is that handsome cook that you are not married to keeping himself?"

"He's in the kitchen breathlessly awaiting your order to arrive so he can cook it to perfection just for you," Cameo said, looking at Jane for her order.

"I'll have the same," Jane said, her eyes widening in fear of a cat fight right there in public.

"You got a problem with me?" Millie asked bluntly.

"No ma'am. Your food will be out soon. We're a little backed up, but I'll bring your Dr. Peppers and you can sip on them while you wait," Cameo chalked up the first round in her favor. She wasn't interested in Sonny Johnson, but she'd sure run interference for Millie's poor old husband.

"Make this one especially thick with onions and give them both extra fries," Cameo told Sonny as she clothes pinned the order to the line in front of the other orders.

"Governor of the great state of Oklahoma eating with us today?" He asked.

"No, your *petit jolie fille* from last night awaits your special culinary arts. The one that squeezed your thigh under the table cloth while she looked right at her husband. She'd like for you to serve it up to her, too, and be sure to roll the sleeves of your tee shirt a little higher so she can see that magnificent tattoo," Cameo said.

Sonny rolled his eyes toward the ceiling. "My little pretty girl, huh? So you speak a little French with a touch of Cajun? You from Louisiana or do you spend some time in France?"

"Ain't damn likely. So you know a little French too. Take it in high school or when you were in the penitentiary?" She snapped.

"I do believe that would be delving into the past. What's funny is that I know a man in . . . well, it doesn't matter where . . . just that he says those three words with that exact inflection," Sonny threw two burger patties on the grill and shook a generous amount of onion rings on top of them.

"What three words? *Petit jolie fille?*" She grabbed

three red plastic baskets filled with burgers and fires, balancing them on her arm.

"No, *ain't damn likely*," he said. "And you can serve Millie. I like her husband too well to get involved with that piece of real estate."

"Sayin' if you didn't like Wally, you might?" Cameo asked.

"Sayin' it ain't damn likely," Sonny said. "And if you want a cook for the rest of the month, you'll take care of it, Cameo."

"Ah, are we threatening the boss?" She asked.

"No ma'am, just statin' facts," he said.

A bus load of church kids going to Falls Creek stopped outside the cafe just as the lunch rush had begun to wane. They crowded into the cafe right after Millie paid for Jane's and her own lunch. Cameo told them to come back soon but her heart wasn't in the words. She grabbed a fresh order pad and started making rounds as the booths began to fill up. She didn't even see Millie and Jane slip back to the kitchen.

"Hi you handsome old thing," Millie leaned against the door frame and blinked seductively at Sonny. "It does a woman's heart good to see a man in the kitchen."

"Well, then you should have a good heart," Sonny quipped. He'd quit this job as soon as the day was finished. He'd told Cameo to take care of it but oh, no. She'd probably sent the vulture and the glorified nun back to the kitchen just to annoy him. Well, if she wanted annoyance, he'd show her a healthy dose. Let her cook and run the front at the same time. That should be payback enough.

"Touchy today are we?" Millie batted her long, fake,

jet black eyelashes at him, and fluffed a mane of bleached blond hair over her shoulder.

"Careful. You'll get some of that hair in my food and I'll get fired," he said.

"Oh, honey, I'll give you a job if Cameo fires you. You just come around about two o'clock when I get back from the tanning bed and I'll give you a summer job in my yard. You can take care of the mowing and weeding and every other beautiful thing at my place," she said, fanning her face with the back of her hand and never taking her eyes from him.

"I don't think I'd want to train for that job. I just got this one down real good," he said in a slow Texas drawl.

"Why, I almost forgot to tell you. I saw this man on the ten o'clock news last night from Texas. He sounded just like you when he talked. Something about some big oil merger down there where the two biggest companies are joining forces to make one humongous enterprise. Man had silver hair but he had a dimple in his chin like yours and looked a whole lot like you," Millie said.

"They say everyone has a twin somewhere," Sonny almost swallowed his tongue. So Murray County, Oklahoma was so far back in the woods, no one would ever figure out he was really Will Dalhart, would they? Did his father and Red Marshall forget about the media, the modern day of cable television, computers, and telephones?

"Oh, he wasn't nearly as handsome as you. And a lot older. Like maybe he could be your father or your uncle or something. But then if you had relatives like that you sure wouldn't be working in a place like this, would you?" She edged closer to him.

"Orders by the dozen," Cameo pushed through the swinging doors into the kitchen area to find Millie flirting and Jane blushing. "What are you doing back here?" She pinned the orders to the line and glared at Millie at the same time.

"Oh, darlin', I was just giving your cook here another option should you be mean and fire him because one of my hairs got into the food. I offered him a job as my gardener for the whole summer," Millie said.

"I got a better idea. If you want to spend some time around him, why don't you grab a potato peeler and get busy. Looks to me like we're about out of French fries and every one of these orders is for an onion burger basket. Bet you could really get to see a lot of my cook in these close quarters. There's aprons on the nail beside the back door. I wouldn't want you to get potato white all over that expensive silk blouse," Cameo rushed back out the doors to take another half dozen orders from loud teenagers.

Millie set her jaw in anger and followed her out into the dining room. The day she peeled a potato for any reason other than to show off at a social would be the day that pigs flew and hundred dollar bills fell from the clouds in a rain storm.

"Leaving?" Cameo wrote fast and furious as eight kids crowded in a four person booth told her just how they wanted their burgers cooked.

"Of course I'm leaving," Millie said.

"And I thought we had some help. We'd pay you minimum wage and you could eat supper free," Cameo didn't miss a word the kids said.

"The day I dirty my hands in a place like this will never come," Millie said through clenched teeth.

"Some of us have more class than a two bit waitress like you. You're just lucky Joyce saw fit to give you a job while she's on vacation. What do you do for her anyway? Make her coffee in the mornings? I can't see you being smart enough to do much more than that. And God knows you don't have the beauty for window dressing."

"Yep, I just make coffee for Joyce," Cameo said. "But me and Mr. Coffee do make a mean cup of coffee so I suppose my job isn't in too much jeopardy."

Millie huffed out of the cafe, Jane behind her like a little trained puppy on a leash.

"So you quitting at the end of the day?" Cameo asked as she pinned six more orders on the line.

"I'll give you one more chance to keep those women out of my kitchen then I just might become a gardener," he said, glancing over at Cameo while he slapped more burgers on the grill. Sweat beaded up under her nose. Those thick glasses magnified the dark circles under her eyes. The twelve hour shifts were taking their toll on her as much as they did him. He'd never leave her in a lurch, but he'd never let her know that, either.

"Deal. Even if I have to put a pad lock on the door," she said.

He shook the grease from the bottom of a basket of fries and tossed them into an empty foot long hot dog container to drain. By the time he assembled six burgers most of the excess grease was soaked up into the container, and he filled the plastic baskets full, shaking a generous amount of salt over all six.

"Order up!" He helped her line the baskets up her arm, wondering the whole time how she managed to get from kitchen to dining room without dropping half of them. She had to have waitressed since she was a young teenager.

A kid plugged several coins into the juke box, adding more noise to the already dull roar in the dining room. Toby Keith sang something about Marshall Dillon asking Miss Kitty to marry him. He sang about the fact he should've been a cowboy, stealing young girls' hearts and singing campfire songs. She listened to the words of the song as she delivered orders to kids who didn't even look at her. How often had she done the same thing in a restaurant? Never thinking about the waiter or waitress who kept her glass filled or made sure her food was the right temperature when it was served.

A booth full of young girls began to sway with the slow music playing next on the juke box. Cameo recognized it as "All Over Me" by Blake Shelton, a relatively new artist she really liked. Millie wondered if she'd ever love anyone enough to crawl on her knees for the whole world to see how much she loved them. She doubted it.

As quickly as the Strawberry Moon had turned into a mad house of noisy kids going to Falls Creek for a week, it was suddenly a tomb of quietness. The bus pulled out from the parking lot and there wasn't a single soul left in the cafe. Cameo bussed the tables, tossing the liners from the red plastic baskets into the trash can. At least Sonny was a good cook. There wasn't one fry or bread crumb left in most of the baskets. By the time she had the tables sprayed and wiped down, the floor swept, and the finger prints removed from the glass door, Sonny pushed open the doors and carried out two large salads in real glass bowls.

"Bless your heart. I'm so hungry I could eat both of those," she said.

"Ain't damn likely," he grinned.

Her heart melted at the sight of the dimple deepening in his chin. He set the salads down at their favorite booth and went back to the fountain to make two iced teas. By the time he returned she'd begun without him. Blake Shelton finished singing "All Over Me," and Sonny wondered if he'd ever find someone who'd affect him like that. Sonny had bought that CD a couple of weeks before and wished he'd brought his collection and even the portable player with him. At least he could have music at night instead of *Land Before Time*.

George Jones's voice filled the room singing, "He Stopped Loving Her Today."

"One of my father's favorites," Sonny said before he thought.

"Oh, a bit of past here? Well, since you showed me a bit of yours, I'll return the favor. It's my father's also," she said.

Guess it doesn't matter if a father is an oil baron or a redneck farmer, they can like the same music, he thought.

"Guess your father loved a woman like that," she said between bites.

"Guess so," Sonny remembered his mother and the fit she'd thrown when he came home with the temporary tattoo and the way his father mourned her when she was gone.

The mood was somber as they both lost themselves in memories of their deceased mothers. The song finished, but the next voice out of the juke box was George Jones too. He sang about the woman who was the rock that he leaned on and how she took him in and made him everything he was and he wasn't going to throw her away.

Sonny wondered whose rock Cameo would be some-day. In her social circles, thirty was getting long in the tooth for catching a man. Most of her friends, like the young married women at the church social, had been married for years and years. Come to think of it, most of his were too. All but Felicia, and her time as the last remaining single woman in the crowd was getting short.

Cameo was suddenly homesick. If she'd been in France, shopping and relaxing, she wouldn't have thought once about her father, but a simple juke box sit-ting in the back of a hamburger joint out on Highway 77 south of Davis had brought him to mind. It wasn't breaking rules to call him from the trailer phone. Maybe she'd do that tonight.

Brad Paisley sang about mud on the tires. Then Darryl Worley filled the empty cafe with his song about a Tennessee river run. They ate in silence, listening to the words of the country songs. Then just as they were finishing the last sip of tea in their glasses, Lee Ann Womack's voice piped out of the juke box with "I Hope You Dance."

Sonny stood up and held out his hand. "May I have this dance, boss lady?"

"Oh, he cooks and he dances too?" She said, taking off her apron and dropping it on the table beside her plate. "Will wonders never cease?"

She fit into his arms as perfectly as if she'd been cre-ated for that purpose. He pulled her into his chest and inhaled the combination of onions and shampoo lingering in her strawberry blond hair. Peace. That's what he felt with Cameo in his arms.

Lee Ann sang about one door closing and another opening and asked for the promise that fate would be given a fighting chance. Would Cameo give Sonny a fighting chance if things were different? She couldn't answer the question, nor did she have time to do so.

The little bell above the door began to tingle and Millie rushed in, stopping in the middle of the floor just as the song ended. "Well, well, so that's the reason you keep your claws out where the drifter is concerned. You've got designs on him for yourself, do you?"

"That would certainly be none of your business, now would it?" Cameo could've beat the woman stone cold to death with a red plastic burger basket for ruining the nicest moment she'd had since she'd left Dallas.

"Hummph," Millie snorted and stormed out the door.

"Thank you for a lovely dance," Cameo said graciously.

"You are quite welcome, Miss Johnson," Sonny bowed elegantly at the waist. "And here comes another bus load of kids. Oh, well, the juke box has played out. Maybe they'll at least entertain us with another round of good old country music. Don't let Millie rile you."

"Rile me? If anger were bullets she'd be bleeding on the floor," Cameo said. "Just don't be running off to be her gardener before the month is out." She moaned as the first batch of kids came through her clean door.

"Ain't damn likely," he grinned, picked up their dirty dishes, and disappeared into the kitchen.

"Holy smoke," she mumbled. "That's the way Daddy says those words. Surely he's not ever met my father." She shook her head. Couldn't be. That would be too much coincidence in the world and Ivy Cameo Elizabeth Marshall did not believe in coincidence, or luck either.

Chapter Six

The sun was bright and a good hot breeze blew strands of hair across Cameo's face as she hung bed sheets on the line to dry that Sunday afternoon. If she hadn't been so rotten angry with Sonny she might have washed his sheets along with hers, but he could do them himself when he got home from his fabulous game of golf with the guys. She could just spit every time she thought about him out there on the golf course and hoped it turned out to be only slightly bigger than a postage stamp with a swamp all around it to steal his golf balls. She even hoped Millie decided to skip the shopping trip and play since Wally was going and that could be her excuse, but Cameo couldn't see Millie doing anything that might produce a bead of sweat. Most assuredly not spending her only day off stripping beds and vacuuming the carpets.

It had all started the night before when Twyla and her husband came into the cafe for a burger. Then Jane and her husband stopped in and had tea. Before long Wally and Millie joined the group and the men started talking about a golf game on Sunday right after church. They invited Sonny to go along and even offered to let him use someone's clubs. The women made it up between them that they'd all go to Norman to go shopping. Dillards had a big sale going and there was this quaint little Mexican place just up the road at Moore where they planned to have lunch.

Sonny had asked where the golf course was located and Wally told him just over in Sulphur then gave him a bit of history. Sulphur was the Murray County seat and was a little bit bigger town than Davis. Yes, they would pick him up right after twelve, soon as church let out, so he wouldn't have to ride his motorcycle over there.

There was no way Norman or Moore was inside the confines of Murray County and Cameo sure couldn't tell the ladies why she really couldn't go shopping with them. So she'd pleaded off with the fact she had to do some cleaning and laundry since it was her only day off work. But now Sonny was gone and she could just chew up rail road spikes and spit out nails thinking about it all. Even with Millie's barbs, a day out with the girls would have been wonderful.

Sheets on the line, she took her attitude back to the house and dragged out the vacuum from the living room closet. She couldn't even remember the last time she'd run a vacuum cleaner. Must have been back in her college days, she reflected as she plugged the machine in and then spent ten minutes trying to find the power button. By the time she finished her bedroom and pushed the heavy machine out into the living room, she had a whole new respect for her cleaning lady.

She threw herself down on the sofa and stared at the vacuum as if it were the devil reincarnated. Taking off her glasses and squinting, she could imagine the cord being a long forked tail and the handle a skinny head with a wicked smile. Holy smoke, but she was sitting on a pity pot. It was time to get off it. Time to think about being superwoman and winning the bet.

Music was what she needed but there didn't seem to be any sign of a stereo system anywhere. She put her glasses back on and scanned the bookcase and bar separating the living room from the kitchen. Beside the evil vacuum, there was a small television with a stash of videos on the bottom shelf. Nothing in either of those rooms, so she went to her bedroom to see if there might be a portable CD player hiding somewhere. She checked the bottom shelves of both night stands and found nothing. She opened the walk-in closet and checked the shelves. Nothing there either. But there was a cabinet at the back side of the closet with doors on it. She opened it to find a CD player, turn table for old 33 rpm records and an assortment of both albums and CD's organized in the shelves below the turn table. She picked up a George Jones CD and put it in the player and was surprised to hear the music filter through both the bedroom and the living room. Looking up, she saw the speakers imbedded into the ceiling in both rooms.

"Well, well," she almost smiled. "So April does like music, and it appears country is her favorite. I do get a miracle today after all, thank you very much."

She turned it up loud enough to make the folks in

Green Hill Cemetery, located on up the road, start tapping their toes, and attacked the house work with anger induced energy. George Jones reminded her of her father and their conversation on Tuesday night. He'd been in touch with Joyce and was already in flames when he answered the phone that night, ranting and raving about coming to Davis and taking her straight to Austin, himself if she didn't get rid of the drifter she'd installed in April's house.

He should have known better than to tell her what she had to do. That had made her dig her heels in and argue with him even harder. No, she would not get rid of her cook. He'd been the perfect gentleman and besides they were both so tired at the end of the day, they were content to go to their very separate bedrooms and sleep until morning. She'd fought with her father like a tiger, telling him that the only reason he wanted her to get rid of Sonny Johnson was because he didn't want to lose the bet, but he had better get out his check book and bite the bullet. She had decided on a bright red Cadillac Seville with all the bells and whistles offered.

"And that's that," she said aloud as the George Jones CD finished at the same time her vacuuming job did. She slipped in a Travis Tritt CD next and threw herself down on the floor of the bedroom, hooked her toes under the bed frame, and began doing sit ups. After a couple hundred crunches she figured she'd have at least half her anger worked off.

Travis was her ultimate favorite singer and entertainer. More than once she'd flown half way across the world to see him in concert. She'd declared she'd watch him sing from any angle. From the front with those pretty eyes and smile which wasn't totally unlike Sonny's. From the back with that fanny tucked into those tight fitting jeans. Again, not unlike the way Sonny filled out his blue jeans.

"Don't Give Your Heart to a Rambler," shook the rafters of the house as she worked up a sweat doing sit ups. "That's for sure," she panted as she listened to the words of the song. That's sure enough what Sonny was . . . a rambler. And he'd be riding on north on that Harley in a couple of weeks. He'd been right up front in the beginning and told her he'd only sit still a month. He was a drifter, a rambler, and like Travis sang, she shouldn't fall in love with a rambler.

"Love," she hissed. "Me falling in love with someone who is nothing but a cook? It ain't damn likely for sure."

By the time the next song finished she was too tired to be angry. All she could think about was a long, soaking bath and a good thick romance book. She ran the tub full of water, added grape scented bubble bath she found in the rack on the wall above the faucets, and lowered her body into the bath. Then she remembered she hadn't picked up her novel. It was just too much trouble to get out and find it, so she leaned back in the tub and let the bubbles gather up around her chest. Travis sang, "Here's a Quarter, Call Someone Who Cares." Maybe she'd better get a whole roll of quarters and start passing them out. Two to Joyce. A dozen to Red Marshall. Ten or fifteen to Millie. Maybe even one to tuck inside Sonny's tight blue jeans when he picked up his last paycheck from the Strawberry Moon.

Then Travis sang "Bible Belt," and Cameo began to giggle. Surely Travis had played the Arbuckle Ballroom and danced with Millie. Then he went home and wrote the song just for her. It talked about her being a looker and having a body made for sin. "Yep, that's our Millie, going and breaking the laws of the Bible belt," she said aloud.

She fell asleep in the middle of the next song but when the music clicked off she awoke with a start. The squeak of the front door echoing through the stark silence and a prickle of fear sent an adrenaline rush through her body.

"That you Sonny?" She called from the bathroom, suddenly aware of the fact the bathroom door as well as the bedroom door were both wide open.

"It's me. I'm going to take a shower and . . . did you wash my sheets?" He yelled from the living room.

"No, and stay out of here. I'm not your maid. You can wash your own sheets or sleep on them dirty. Your choice," she yelled back, easing out of the tub and wrapping a big towel around her body. "But if you want clean ones tonight you'd better get them on the line before long. It's already four o'clock."

She hid in the bathroom until she heard the door slam to the bedroom he used and then hurried across the floor to shut her own door. She started the Travis Tritt CD again, and hoped Sonny hated the man's singing.

Sonny shed his sweaty clothing and breathed a sigh of relief. There on the top of the unmade bed was his journal. When he saw sheets flapping on the line, he'd been afraid she'd been in his room and read the journal. Each and every day he'd filled it with something more about his job and Cameo being the woman he was going to convince to marry him. Of course, he had no intentions of marrying the waitress—even if they did dance well together that one time.

Travis Tritt's voice filled the whole trailer, quite loudly. So Cameo had found a stereo and it was piped into more than one room. He patted his foot to the music and stripped the sheets from the twin sized bed. Lord, but he'd be glad to get home to his king sized bed. He'd been to every concert Travis had done and owned every CD he'd made. The one Cameo was playing had been produced in 1991, more than a decade ago, when Sonny was in his early twenties and fresh out of college. Back when Sonny had long hair and a beard just like Travis and reveled in the fact that he looked somewhat like the country music artist. Both of them had aged. Travis's music got better and better and Sonny climbed the oil corporation ladder of success.

Sonny listened to Travis sing about nothing short of dying that's worse than being left alone. Would Sonny feel like that when he left Cameo behind after he'd proposed to her? One thing was for sure, he'd best be buttering her up tonight because she was surly as an rangy old bull this morning when he left to play golf with the guys. She could've gone shopping with the girls, but oh, no, she had to be a martyr and do housework all day. It wasn't a sin to let the vacuuming and dusting go for another week, but evidently where she'd been raised cleaning and bed changing had to be done once a week or the sun wouldn't come up the next morning.

He showered, towel dried his hair, and shaved, applying a generous amount of shaving lotion to his face, then wiping the rest on his hairy chest. With the towel wrapped securely around his waist he snuck down the hall and into his Pepto pink room. Dressed in freshly washed, if not creased and ironed, jeans, and a white tee shirt, he carefully combed his hair back. He needed a hair cut, but it would have to wait until he got to Austin. Maybe he'd let it grow out again, and maybe he'd grow a beard, he eyed himself in the mirror.

Not much looked like Travis these days. Life had bit them both. Little wrinkles graced the corners of his eyes and there were commas from the corners of his nose to his mouth. Will Dalhart, alias Sonny Johnson, wasn't getting any younger. Travis's words about looking to find true love filled the air around him. "Will, old boy, you'd better be looking for a woman looking to find the same thing before you get so old there's no one out there except old women eye-balling your bank account. You need to talk to Felicia," he whispered.

"House looks good. Smells clean and nice. Let me take you out to an early supper," he said without looking at Cameo when he walked into the living room.

She was cuddled up in the corner of the sofa, her nose in a thick book. A white towel turban kept her wet hair at bay. She smelled faintly like grape flavored Kool-Aid. She cocked her eyes over the top of the book at him. Now that was just like a real husband. Go off and play golf, then come home and say the house smells nice. Let me take you out to supper. How romantic!

"You been working all day and neither of us wants to cook. No one invited us to a church social tonight. Can't say as I would go even if they had since everyone knows we're not married now. The guys say they've got some unmarried friends they'd like to fix you up with," he grabbed the remote and plopped down in a worn recliner. He found a sports channel and settled in to watch it while his sheets finished washing.

"Ain't that nice," she crooned icily.

"What on earth are you so mad about anyway?"

"What am I mad about? Think, Sonny. Use the two sane brain cells God gave you to rub together and make a thinking process. I've been stuck here doing chores while you've been out playing all day," she said.

"You could have gone shopping and to lunch with the girls," he countered.

"I'd rather eat worms than spend the day with Millie hanging on every word about you," she said.

"Jealous?" He grinned.

Merciful heavens, he did look like Travis when he smiled. How had she never noticed that before? *No he doesn't. It's just the fact you're reading a hot, steamy romance and listening to Travis*, her conscience told her bluntly. "Me jealous? You got to be kidding. You don't see any green on me do you?"

"Just wishing, I guess. How about supper? Take you down to that little Mexican place on Main Street if you want. I'll even pick up the check. How's that for penance for having a good time when you couldn't? Of course, there's the Subway or the Sonic if you want a choice. The two little cafes off Main, Dougherty Diner and Main Street Restaurant, are both closed on Sunday just like the Strawberry Moon," he said, wondering if he would ever get her to say she'd marry him in just two more weeks.

"Okay, and I'm ordering the most expensive thing on the menu," she said. "So you better get ready to drop a bunch of your hard earned money."

"Fair enough," he said.

"How was the golf game?" She asked.

"Pretty good. Nice little course over there. Wally whipped us all, but it was an enjoyable day. I just started the washing machine so my sheets should be done in half an hour. I'll put them on the line and do my load of towels in the morning before we go to work. Put on that fancy dress you wore last week and we'll turn the town upside down," he grinned again.

Her heart melted in spite of the warnings from her mind.

She nodded and went back to reading, turning several pages before she laid the book down and meandered toward her bedroom. Hurriedly, she threw off the faded terry cloth robe she'd borrowed from the hook on the back of the bathroom door, and commenced to getting dressed for a date. A real one, even if it was with a drifter from nowhere going to nowhere. There was a god in heaven after all.

She carefully applied her makeup, dried her hair, and twisted it up into a French roll, letting the curls escape at the top. She slipped into the dress, adjusted the straps, and slid her feet into the sandals. If only she didn't have to wear the glasses she'd feel better about herself. But the opthamologist had said a month. By the time she got to Austin she could throw them in the drawer and put her contacts back in, and it wouldn't be a day too soon.

He whistled under his breath when she came back into the living room. "Now don't you look lovely," he said. It wasn't a lie. Cameo was a looker all right. A lovely lady even with the glasses that kept sliding down her aristocratic nose. Long, shapely legs. One of those peaches and cream complexions his mother talked about when she was still living. Yes, given another time and place, he might have even dated her seriously. But time, fate, and chance hadn't blessed him with such a miracle.

"Thank you, kind sir, but compliments will not get you out of paying for my supper. Shall we go? You can drive," she tossed the keys to the Lexus at him.

He caught them midair, amazed that he'd won her trust enough that she'd let him drive the car. He might have a chance of making her accept his proposal after all. Should he get on one knee and do it up right the night before the month was over? Or should he do something original to sweep her off her feet? One thing was for sure, he would need a ring. And he'd have to buy it in Murray County. Thank goodness there was a jewelry store on Main Street, but how in the world was he going to get down there and purchase a ring during the daylight hours? He frowned as he opened the door for Cameo, trying to plan a way to take care of the matter.

"Already regretting asking me out to supper?" She asked.

"Not at all. I'm right proud to be dating you," he said.

"Hey, wait a minute," she said as she slid into the passenger seat of the fancy car. "This is just two people who work together going for supper. You are not dating me."

He cocked his head to one side. "Dating has to do with the present, darlin'. We don't have to reveal the past to do that."

"You are impossible," she laughed.

They sat in one of the booths along the side of the

cafe. Small town atmosphere filled the authentic Mexican restaurant. Folks came in, stopped to visit with any and everyone, some even including Cameo and Sonny in their rounds, who nibbled on tortilla chips and freshly made salsa while they waited on enchiladas. Just as the young waitress brought them their food, Millie and Wally opened the front door.

"Well, speak of the devil and he shall appear," Sonny said glibly.

"Or his sister!" Cameo shut her eyes, wishing desperately that when she opened them Millie and Wally would be gone. Wishes were not granted that hot summer evening because Millie made a bee line for their booth. Before she got there, Sonny reached across the table and covered Cameo's hand with his.

"Oh, so you two are together. I thought so after seeing you dancing in the Moon, and you telling us that cock and bull story about never seeing him before. What else did you lie about?" Millie asked rudely.

"Millie come home telling me about her lunch and it set my teeth on edge for some Mexican food," Wally said, ignoring his wife completely.

"Then you'd better find a table. Looks like it's filling up in a hurry," Sonny said, looking right into Cameo's eyes without blinking.

"I guess it is," Wally punched Sonny on the shoulder and winked.

"What was that all about?" Cameo said between clenched teeth.

"Protecting my friendship with Wally. That wife of his is pure poison," he said, but he didn't take his hand from hers, nor did she slide hers out of his.

If he could protect his friendship, then she could use

him to get back at Millie. Lord Almighty, but that woman was surely a dose of arsenic, just like he'd said.

They finished their meal, talking about the Strawberry Moon, their newly found friends, how that Davis seemed to be a prosperous, growing little town with lots of personality, and winding up with a discussion about taking time next Sunday to visit the antique shops on Main Street.

Back at the house, he kept the keys to the Lexus long enough to open the door to the trailer before he handed them back to her. When she reached for them, he deliberately dropped them on the carpet. Both of them bent at the same time to retrieve them, their faces merely inches apart. In the darkness, they stood in slow motion, his hand holding tightly to her hand holding the keys. Without a word, he moved in for the kiss. She leaned into him, liking the way he brushed the hair away from her face before he kissed her. A new Caddy with all the bells and whistles didn't compare to what she experienced when his lips touched hers. Music played in her heart, a sweet melody that reminded her of the green, green grasses in Scotland, a lovely haunting sound that told her in the space of one kiss that she was a fool if she didn't stop this in its tracks.

Nothing in Sonny's thirty three years had prepared him for the jolt of pure desire that filled his whole body when he wrapped his arms around Cameo Johnson and kissed her. Convincing her to marry him shouldn't be difficult. A couple of those kisses and he might have to convince himself he wasn't sincere. But Will Dalhart couldn't take a waitress home to meet his father. It would take more water than what had fallen upon the earth during Noah's day to put out the flames if he pulled a stunt like that.

"What was that all about?" She asked, pulling away and turning on the lights to burn out the sweet darkness surrounding them.

"That was the end of a date with Sonny Johnson," he said. "Good night, Cameo." He left her standing in the living room and went out the back door to retrieve his sheets.

"What is this?" He moaned when he saw the white streak of bird dropping streaking across Barbie's eyes. This would bring anyone back to the reality of the moment, he thought. Just a friendly reminder of the real caliber woman Cameo Johnson is. A waitress living in a house with a broken clothes dryer she couldn't afford to have fixed, who had to hang sheets on the line where birds could use them for a bathroom. He carried the sheets carefully into the house, careful that the still-soft bird mess did not touch any other place, used a wash cloth from the bathroom to remove the streak, and then made his bed, hoping all the time that the wet spot would soon dry, or else he'd be hugging the wall like it was a brother.

He picked up his journal and wrote:

Day thirteen: Job still going. Today I played golf with some of the guys I met at the church social and who've been coming into the Strawberry Moon. Inside Murray County. Romance progressing right along. In two more weeks, I shall propose and she will accept.

Chapter Seven

Monday was a long hectic day with five vans of kids stopping on their way to Falls Creek. After two weeks, Cameo had figured out their schedule. On Monday they checked into the cabins out there in the mountains. On Saturday they checked out. During that time they most likely had lessons, time for socializing, and church every night. But on the way down, the Strawberry Moon appeared to be the place to stop for lunch. Not that she minded the business, no siree! Now that she knew Mondays and Saturdays were the busiest days of the week, she could be better prepared.

Though she didn't have time to speak to Sonny other than to discuss burgers and corn dogs, the kiss from the night before kept playing through her mind over and over again and nothing she did seemed to be able to turn it off. At the end of the day, they quietly walked out the back door of the cafe.

"Hey, look," Cameo pointed up at the full moon.

"It's June and that's a full moon, so it must be a strawberry moon."

"I guess it would be," Sonny nodded, trying desperately not to think about the strawberry blond beside him who'd turned his world upside down with one kiss.

The hot, still night air smothered a body without stirring a bit and the central air conditioning unit buzzed an invitation. However, Cameo didn't want to go inside. She handed Sonny the key and sat down on the bottom porch step, took her shoes off, and wiggled her tired toes in the grass which needed mowing. She mentally checked off the responsibilities she'd agreed to for her new Caddy. Mowing the lawn wasn't one of them, so April and Joyce could come home to a yard that could be baled and sold for hay for all she cared. The ankle deep, green grass tickled her bare feet, bringing back memories of when she was a child and running through the grass at the ranch in the spring time. She missed those days when everything in her life was simple. When she didn't work twelve hour days in an office and wear shoes from before daylight until midnight. When she wasn't thirty with the tick tock of her biological clock playing loudly in her ears. Maybe she needed to throw the clock out in the yard and make arrangements for the photographer to come take her picture for the old maid's hall of fame.

She rolled the kinks from her neck and thought about going inside for a long, hot bath. But the trailer was as confined as her mind. Outside there were wide open spaces and she didn't have to think. Just appreciate. Just a few more minutes, and then she'd go back inside to face the routine. But now, right now, she was going to do something she hadn't done since she was a child. She threw herself down on her back in the middle of the yard, stretched lazily, put her hands behind her head, and looked up at the twinkling stars, a blanket of diamond dust on a puffy velvet comforter.

Before she could blink twice Sonny was beside her, his muscular frame close enough she could feel the heat from his body invading her space. "Scoot over," she demanded.

"Why? Do I smell like onions and grease?" He asked.

"No, it's a hot night and you are ninety eight point six degrees of more heat. I don't mind sharing my grass or my stars with you, but I'm not absorbing your heat," she said without taking her eyes from the sky.

"Did you see that?" He asked as he put a few more inches between them.

"What? Did I miss a comet?" She tried to cover the whole sky with one glance.

"No, fireflies. Ever run around in the evening catching them when you were a kid? Momma would poke holes in a jar lid and I'd make a lightning bug lantern. Sometimes I'd even get a bit sadistic and smear the yellow stuff on their flickering tails on my cheeks and make myself into a modern day painted up Indian on the war path," he said.

"Of course I caught lightning bugs. Kids don't live in . . ." she stammered, almost saying Dallas, Texas. "They don't live in this area without growing up with lightning bugs."

"Ever miss those carefree days?" He asked.

"Of course, but I wouldn't go back to them and have to live through the years between the time when I made myself into a sparkling princess with a lightning bug glittery crown around my forehead until now," she said.

"Why?" He propped up on an elbow so he could better see her face, lit up by the big, round strawberry moon.

"Because the experiences I've been through have made me the woman I am today, and that's fringing on talking about the past, Mr. Sonny Johnson," she said.

"Want to throw the barriers down and really get to know each other? Past mistakes. Future plans. All of it?" He asked.

"No, I do not," she said. That would mean telling him who she really was and finding out who he was. For now, one kiss was enough to set her mind in a whirlwind of crazed thoughts and ideas; her body into a tumble of emotions she didn't even like to admit. Knowing that Sonny was truly mixed up in something shady and sent away to hide out was more than her mind or body could endure. No, she'd rather keep him as a plain old fry cook and roommate for another two weeks. After which, in a few years, she'd remember the month she spent at the Strawberry Moon with a certain longing. Not totally unlike the times when she chased lightning bugs on a hot summer night on a ranch outside Dallas, Texas.

"Why?" He asked after a few minutes of wondering if he'd be breaking the rules if he did tell her who he was or what she'd do with the information that he was a rich oil baron.

"Because it would cost me too much," she said.

"Let's go swimming," he said.

"Sonny, it's ten thirty and we have to get up early," she told him.

"And it's only two miles out to Turner Falls Park. Wally told me about it and I passed it when I drove into town the day you hired me. If we give up our run tomorrow morning and call swimming our exercise, we could sleep until eight o'clock," he said.

"Sorry, idea is good but you don't swim at Turner Falls this late. Against the rules," she said. "I heard the kids talking about how they don't let folks swim after ten out there."

He sighed so loud she felt sorry for him, but it would be a waste of time to don different clothes and ride out there, only to find what she already knew. She sat up, wrapped her arms around her legs, and watched the flickering lights of the fireflies. She remembered an evening when Joyce came to play. They were about eight years old and they'd chased fireflies, played in a tent made of a sheet draped over a wire Red ran from one pecan tree to another, and then just before bed had a glorious water fight with the two garden hoses.

By the light of the moon she saw a green hose coiled up neatly above the water faucet at the end of the trailer beside the porch. On the other end of the trailer was another one. If she sprayed Joyce in the face now, when they were both thirty years old, her friend slash assistant slash confidant would have her committed to the nearest mental facility. That's what two weeks of working in the Strawberry Moon got her. Thoughts of water fights and lightning bug lanterns. Letting one kiss, passionate as it was, invade every thought for a whole day.

However, tonight was one of those strange nights. One when there was very little past, no future at all, only the present. The present when Cameo was a waitress at the Strawberry Moon and Sonny was a cook. So if Sonny wanted to be wet, she could sure oblige his fantasy.

"You going in already?" He asked when she started toward the house.

"In a few minutes," she said.

He shut his eyes and wished he did know her background. She talked like an educated woman, worked hard like she was used to it, but there was no way she was anything more than a waitress. No one with any kind of credentials would be working twelve hour shifts at a burger joint in a little resort town in southern Oklahoma. *You are*, his conscience pricked.

But I'm here on a bet, on a mission to show Red and my father that the molds weren't broken when they got rich. I can work as hard as either one of them, he reminded himself. *But*, his brow furrowed in deep thought, *what if she's here on a bet, too? What if she's really not who she says she is?* He shook off that preposterous idea. Two people in one place, both on a bet?

Not damn likely.

A blast of cold water arching through the hot night air splashed him in the face, bringing him into a sitting position as he spat and stammered, trying to figure out where the rain clouds had been hiding. He rubbed his eyes as the water moved down to his chest.

"You wanted to be wet," Cameo giggled from the back of the trailer where she held a hose, her thumb over the nozzle, directing the spray right at him.

He spied the other hose and made a run for it, getting his back wet the whole way. She squealed when he quickly unwrapped enough length to begin the water fight. When the cool water wet down her tee shirt, she sucked air and ran around the end of the trailer still tightly gripping the hose in her possession.

They each had twenty five feet of green garden hose with a bright yellow line. By retreating to the ends of the trailer they could hide from the other one. However, if they wanted to chance a soaking they could sneak twenty five feet down the back side of the trailer and lay in wait for the other to come out of hiding.

"You are a lily livered Indian and I will shoot you dead in your tracks when you show your face," she taunted when she'd crept around the trailer as far as her hose would reach.

"And you are a princess from the planet Venus whom I now blast with my laser gun," he said jumping out and sending a spray of cold water straight into her hair, already hanging in limp curls.

She gave as good as she got for the next half hour when they both called a truce, declaring that neither of them had won, nor lost the garden hose war. Hoses rewound, they sat down on the back porch. The tiredness of the day evaporated in the blasts of water, they were rejuvenated and could have talked all night.

"How old are you, Cameo?" He asked, careful not to sit too close. He was having enough trouble keeping his eyes from all a wet tee shirt did not cover.

"That's not a question you ask a lady," she started to poke him on the arm but kept her hands to herself. After that mind-boggling kiss from the night before, she didn't think touching him would be a good idea. She'd forget she was Ivy Marshall, heir to an oil empire, and go ahead and fall for the rambling man known as Sonny Johnson.

"But I'll tell you if you promise to never breath it to

another soul. I usually require that a person sign an oath in blood squeezed from their pinky finger before I tell my age or weight. Since you're only interested in age, I'll let you get by with your promise," she teased.

"You got my promise. I don't want to know your weight enough to be sticking my finger," he chuckled.

"I was thirty years old a month ago," she said. "And you?"

"Let me have your pinky finger," he held out his hand.

"No," she jumped back as if he held a spider.

"I'm only teasing. I'm thirty three," he said. "And the reason I asked is that I can't remember when I've had so much fun as I've had since I went to work at the Strawberry Moon. Do you think they'd sell us the joint and we could work there forever?"

"Dear Lord, I hope not," she said. "I can't imagine being a waitress the rest of my life. Would you really be content to be a cook forever?"

"Maybe," he shrugged. "I guess thirty and thirty three is a little old for water fights and catching fireflies, isn't it?"

"It was just the moment of the hour," she said. "Fun knows no age, Sonny. Reminiscing isn't bad, either. But let's get real. You're a drifter whose only promised to work at the Moon a month at the most. I've got a job I'll go back to after April and Joyce come home. Our worlds will only mix this month. After that we'd find out who the other one truly is, and who's to say we'd like the person who's not a waitress or a cook? We probably wouldn't even like each other in another setting."

"Are you married?" He asked out of the dark blue night.

"Where did that come from?" She asked right back without answering his question.

"I think that's the only way I wouldn't like you. If you were married and you'd kissed me like you did last night. I couldn't like a woman who cheated on her husband," he said.

"Meanin' you wouldn't kiss Millie like that if she tipped her red lips up to yours?" She asked.

"Meanin' I would not," he said. "Are you married?"

"No, Sonny, I'm not married. Never have been, much to my father's aggravation. He'd like a yard full of grandkids to chase fireflies and paint their faces with the glow from their tails. And that is all the past you're getting. What about you? You ever been married?" She asked.

"No," he answered with the single syllable word.

"Why?" She asked.

"Because in my line of business you never know if a woman loves you for who you are or what you are, and that, Cameo, is all you get," he said.

"Then I expect we'd better drip across the carpet and call it a night," she stood up and disappeared around the end of the trailer. A few minutes later the back door opened. "Thought I'd be nice and let you in this way. That way you won't leave prints on the carpet too. Good-night, Sonny."

"I'll just sit here a little longer. Thanks for opening the door. 'Night, Cameo," he said.

She dropped her wet clothing in a heap beside the bathtub and ran a warm bubble bath. Tomorrow she was going to forsake her morning run. She was going to sleep until eight o'clock and she was going to squelch all those feelings running rampant in her heart. Sonny

Johnson had all but admitted he was a questionable character when he said why he wasn't married. What woman would marry a man for what he was? One who wanted the notoriety of being married to a member of the mob?

She stayed in the water until after midnight, until the bubbles were flat and the water was lukewarm, but still she couldn't kick the surreal evening from her mind. Thirty years old and laying in the grass and then playing with garden hoses. Women who wore expensive silk suits and shoes that cost more than a week's salary as a waitress didn't squeal and holler in the middle of a water fight. Women who ran the business end of a Texas oil kingdom didn't entertain notions of buying a burger joint and waitressing the rest of their lives.

She dried her body, donned a night shirt, and fell into the bed, staring out the window at the stars. In her Austin penthouse she hoped she had big windows so she could see the stars when she remembered this night.

Warm water beat down on Sonny's broad shoulders for a long time as he stood in the shower. She wasn't married but she was thirty. What was the matter with the male population in southern Oklahoma? Where was she really from anyway? She talked like she came from this area. Either Oklahoma or Texas, but neither Wally nor any of the other guys knew her, so it couldn't be close. From what they'd said, she worked with Joyce who worked somewhere in Dallas. They thought they remembered April saying Joyce had an impressive job at some pretty big firm. That's probably where Cameo worked also. A secretary from a pool much like his own company employed. No doubt at the top of her success ladder and living in one of those apartment complexes covering ground faster than southern kudzu vines. He tried to imagine where she lived; what her real job entailed; did she wear cute little suits and high heeled shoes to work?

He shut off the water and wrapped a towel around his waist. For the first time he didn't even sigh when he shut the door to his room. He stretched out on his twin sized bed with the Barbie sheets and lost himself in thought as he stared blankly out the window at the stars. He didn't even write in his journal. He'd do it tomorrow when everything wasn't such a jumbled mess in his heart.

Chapter Eight

Cameo and Sonny shared a hymn book and sang "Abide With Me," their voices blending with six other people in the tiny little chapel at Turner Falls that Sunday morning at the sunrise service. They'd climbed a long flight of stairs up to the chapel, built of rough wood on the side of a mountain. The congregation, all eight of them, looked more like gypsy vagabonds than church going people. Even the preacher who opened his Bible at the podium, cleared his throat, and began to read scripture, wore jeans and a tee shirt. Wally had told them services were informal at the Falls, but still Cameo felt as if she should at least have something other than flip-flops on her feet.

And there was something even more personal about sharing a hymn book with Sonny than even that kiss they'd shared. It denoted that they were a couple like the other couples around them. Cameo let her mind and eyes wander a bit as she looked at the other couples.

One about their age, the new still on their wedding rings. What a strange place for a honeymoon, yet newly wedded bliss literally oozed out of their pores. Another couple that could have easily been her grandparents if they had still been living. The man with a bald spot in the back of his head and thick glasses, his bony legs sticking out from plaid Bermuda shorts like pipe sticks. The grandmother with a tint of blue in her gray hair, a pair of capris and a tee shirt, and the prettiest soprano voice Cameo had ever heard. The other couple was middle aged, a bit indifferent to each other as if they'd had a fight on their way to services that morning. But they all belonged together; all shared a hymn book. She and Sonny shared the book, but they also shared the distinction of being the only ones who didn't belong together.

The preacher had a message about the here-and-now as opposed to the here-after or the here-before. Cameo, who usually daydreamed at Sunday morning mass, listened to every word and wondered how the man knew what she needed to hear. He finished the short sermon in ten minutes, a kernel of thought-provoking ideas in a nutshell. She and Sonny were the last ones to leave, taking time to stand on the porch a moment and look out over the panoramic view of the mountains.

"Pretty place, isn't it?" He asked. "What do you say we spend the whole day? Hey, looks they're opening that store over there. The Trading Post. We can buy some bologna and bread and a bag of chips. Add a couple of cans of cold soda and we'll be set for a picnic. Want to?"

"Sure," she hated to leave her perch on the small porch. For a moment she reveleled in the here-and-now, relishing the peace of a quiet Sunday morning. "I'm thirsty and today I'm going to splurge and not have a diet drink, but a real one with sugar and caffeine, and I may have a candy bar for breakfast."

"Boy, you were listening when he said all that about not worrying so much about tomorrow, didn't you?" Sonny laughed and started down the steep steps ahead of her.

He hadn't gotten a third of the way down when he heard her gasp and barely turned in time to catch her as she fell into his arms. "Is this a damsel in distress?" He asked.

"No, it's the Murphy's Law as applied to Cameo Johnson," she blushed. Everything she'd touched for two days had gone wrong. If it could go wrong, it did. If it couldn't, it did anyway.

Sonny laughed with her as he set her aright and the two of them went on to the store across the parking lot. It had a bit of everything. Soft drinks, chips, milk, bread, firewood for the campers. Dreamcatchers. Real ones. Before Cameo left she intended to purchase one to hang above her bed in the new Austin penthouse apartment. She'd always loved the ethereal quality of a dreamcatcher, and some of the most breathtaking ones she'd ever seen were hanging right there before her.

And bathing suits. Cameo hadn't even thought about bringing her bathing suit. She'd just figured they'd go to the early morning services, ride back home, and catch up on chores all afternoon. She was so excited she could have kissed the owner or Sonny or maybe both when she saw that rack of bathing suits. She flipped through the hangers holding more than a dozen in a size medium. Deciding on a tankini and a regular bikini, she held them both up for Sonny to see.

"Which one?" She asked.

He rubbed his jaw in mock judgment. "Well, if you were out to get attention, that hot pink bikini ought to do the job. But if you were really my woman or my wife, then the one that covers a little more skin would be my choice. You'll be beautiful in either one. How about this one for me?" He asked, holding up a men's pair of swimming trunks with bright turquoise dolphins on an orange background.

"It's so you," she giggled. "I think I'll go with the tankini. It's orange and we'll match."

"Look out world, here come the Johnsons," he said. "Is there a place where we might change?" He asked the owner.

"Bathrooms are right down there," the man pointed in the direction of the toll gate. "Ya'll from Texas? We get a lot of folks come up from Texas to spend the day or weekend with us," he said as he rang up their purchases and bagged them. "Ya'll have a nice day and come back to see us."

"Thank you. You have a good one too. And we just might come back to these parts someday. It's sure pretty here in the mountains," Sonny said.

"So we're from Texas?" Cameo asked as they covered the ground from the store to the bathrooms.

"Guess I am," Sonny said. "That's what the tag on the motorcycle says anyway."

"Or is the motorcycle just registered there to give you more protection from whoever it is you are hiding from?" She asked, a teasing note in her voice.

"Who do you think I'm hiding from?" He asked.

"Wouldn't know. But today we are Texans up here for the day at the Turner Falls Park, or at least until early afternoon, huh?" She stopped in front of the door with the silhouette of a woman on it.

"That's right. You are a motorcycle momma today, Cameo. Go put on that skimpy bathing suit and we'll have an early morning swim up near the falls and then a long, lazy nap on the sandbar," he told her.

"Don't you be calling me a motorcycle momma or calling my new bathing suit skimpy. The bikini was skimpy. This one will cover a lot more hide," she slapped at him.

"Beat you back to the cycle," he said, shoving open the door with one hand and pulling up his tee shirt with the other.

She caught a flash of soft, dark hair on his chest, and yearned once again to run her fingers though it. Mercy, but she was going to have to get back into the dating world again when she arrived in Austin. Maybe she'd even consent to go out with Chris again, just to get Sonny and all that appealing aura surrounding him out of her mind. She didn't even try to peel out of her clothing at a break neck speed. Sonny had less to take off, less to put back on, and a lot less to adjust. He'd win that race, so why hurry?

He leaned against his motorcycle and waited. He'd folded his things carefully and put them into the small trunk, pushing them to one side so Cameo could store her clothing beside them. When she opened the bathroom door and stepped out into the bright sunlight, his breath caught somewhere in his chest. Why had he ever thought she was anything but stunning? Even with the prescription sunglasses perched on her nose, she looked like a model. All that running surely did keep her in shape and that thing she called a tankini showed off her well toned shape to perfection. He pointed to the trunk and crawled up onto the driver's seat of the big Harley, watching her from the rear view as she meticulously laid her folded things beside his. It seemed sensual, knowing their unmentionables shared space, for some odd reason. Odd, because this was the twenty-first century when women and men cohabited, when the social boundaries had long since been torn down, and when few places had double standards anymore. Take the job in Austin for instance. He'd be working with that barracuda of a woman, Ivy Marshall. It had been said she chewed up men and employees for breakfast and spit them into the unemployment lines. An old maid, pretty as she could be, who was more interested in the oil business than she was any kind of mutual relationship with a member of the male gender. At least that's what he'd heard. He'd looked for a picture of the woman on the cover of any of his oil magazines but found none. Only an article with his picture, Red's, and his father's, on the day the merger became reality.

"Here comes the motorcycle momma," she giggled as she took her place behind him and laced her arms around him, finally getting to sink her fingertips in that wild, curly hair covering his chest. Yes, it was as soft as it looked. She wondered briefly what it would be like to lay her face on his bare chest and listen to his heartbeat.

"Get ready for the first splash," he said, a bit hoarsely, as he gunned the motor and took off with a squeal of tires. He hit the water on the low water bridge where Honey Creek overflowed it by several inches and water sprayed up around them, getting them wet to their waists. Cameo hugged him tighter and squealed at the same time. Sonny Johnson was in heaven.

Honey Creek cut through the park on their left and cabins and houses set off at the foot of the mountain to their right. Cameo didn't miss a thing, but she didn't loosen her hold on Sonny, either. Left as nature made it as much as possible, the park was naturally lovely, especially in the early morning hours. The smell of bacon frying on camp fires floated through the air and she felt Sonny's stomach growl. Would those campers consider selling them bacon, eggs, and fried toast for a hundred dollar bill? She wondered. They reached the end of the road which culminated in a parking lot with a couple of snow cone, candy, and soda vendors.

"So this is where the yellow brick road ends," he said, looking ahead at the foot path toward the falls. He slipped the keys to his cycle in the small pocket inside his swimming trunks.

"Wait a minute, Tonto," she said. "I put our Dr. Peppers and candy bar breakfast in that trunk. Your stomach might stop growling if you open it up. Besides, we'll have our lunch and those two new beach towels along with my skin block. I don't tan but I do burn. Did Wally tell you how far it is from here to the swimming area?"

"No, but it can't be far. Listen, Cameo, you can hear the water rushing over the rocks," he cocked his head off to one side as he retrieved the keys and opened the trunk.

They munched on giant sized Snickers bars and Dr. Peppers as they walked single file toward the noise. What met them around the last bend was absolutely awesome. A seventy-seven foot waterfall tumbling into a natural pool inviting them to dive right in. Everyone else in the park was busy waking up and cooking breakfast, so they had the whole area to themselves right then. There was no wind stirring the scrub oak, dogwoods, and redbuds that morning, and in the stillness Cameo savored the moment, hearing only her own heartbeat and imagining that Sonny's echoed hers even if she couldn't hear it.

"Wow!" He said.

"I agree. I'm going to stretch out right here and do nothing but listen to the noise of that fall for an hour," she said as she found just the right spot and spread her oversized towel in the sand.

"Sounds good to me," he said, doing the same, being careful to keep his towel several inches from hers. "Want me to rub some of that lotion on you?"

"No help needed. I can reach all the places except . . ." her arms couldn't quite get the area between her shoulder blades.

"Hand it here," he said, a grin splitting his handsome face.

She thought she was prepared for the touch of his finger tips touching her skin ever so lightly, like the feathers from the dream catcher, smoothing the lotion over her shoulders. But she wasn't. Tingles did a ballet number up and down her spine, twisting and turning, spinning in the early morning hours as Honey Creek tumbled from the top of the mountain to bottom. One more week, she reminded herself as she shut her eyes but failed to shut out the feelings his finger tips evoked, and she'd be on her way to Austin. Just seven more days. Next Sunday the wager would be won and she'd go home. What Sonny did after that was his own business. Lord, she wished he'd never stop. She wished he would disappear and be gone like the genie in the paranormal romance she'd read last week. She wished she knew more about him. She didn't want to know as much as she knew. How was she ever going to tell him good-bye? She'd forget him in a week. She'd remember him forever. The conflicting emotions were enough to set her nerves on edge. If she didn't get this under control she'd be ordering a gallon bucket of Prozac just to get her through the first weeks of work without Sonny around all the time.

What would he do? She wondered. *Would he go on down the road, drifting into another job maybe hauling hay or cooking in another small cafe somewhere up the highway? Would there be another woman he toyed with for a month? Would he put lotion on her back?* The green head of jealousy raised its ugly head and high color filled Cameo's cheeks as she realized she shouldn't ask such questions. Not even silently in her mind.

"That should do it," he said, so close to her neck that the warmth of breath caressed tender neck skin.

"Thank you," she said, hoping he couldn't hear the breathless quality in her tone.

"What are you thinking about?" He broke the ten minute silence.

"You don't want to know. It would jeopardize our agreement not to have a past," she said.

"Yesterday is history. Tomorrow is a mystery. Today is a present," he said.

"Didn't know you had a poetic soul," she said. "Who's your favorite poet?"

"Rod McKuen. One of his poems says something

about it not mattering who you love but the important thing is that you love," he said, shielding the sun from his eyes with the back of his hand. Did he really believe that? He asked himself. It did matter who he loved. He was Will Dalhart in real life and Cameo was a waitress. She'd faint dead away if she knew who he really was and how much he was worth. Rod McKuen was wrong. It did matter.

"My favorite one of Rod's poems is entitled 'To My Friends Out There in the World,' written about six years ago. I love him, always have. My mother was a special fan of his, met him a couple of times. One of my favorite pictures of her is with him after an appearance in Dallas."

"So you are from Dallas?" He asked.

"Maybe. Maybe not. My mother met Rod McKuen in Dallas and that's yesterday's history lesson. Today I'm following his advice, Sonny. I'm chasing my tail, so to speak. And I'm not giving history lessons or dealing in mystery ones either," she told him. A trail of fading motorcycle exhaust would be the only thing left if Sonny ever found out she was really Ivy Marshall and the up and coming vice president of the new oil merger taking place right now. He'd never be interested in a woman who made fifty times what he did each year. Not swash buckling, handsome Sonny Johnson.

"Who are you Cameo? Who are you really?" He whispered. Was her mother a hippie? Is that where she really got her name?

"I'm the waitress slash manager of the Strawberry Moon Cafe which is closed today because it is Sunday. And a glorious day it is. The present day. I think I'll have a swim and then take a long nap in the sun. Join me?" She asked, opening one eye a slit. Who was Sonny Johnson? Was he really from Texas? Strange, she'd never paid a bit of attention to the license plate on his cycle until today. Or was aware that he might notice the Texas plate on Joyce's Lexus either.

"Of course, and then we shall have a long, lazy nap," he said without looking at her.

They played like children who had no cares or worries, swimming up to the falls, finding a ledge to stand on behind it, and wishing for things that could not be. Like the courage to wrap their arms around each other and see if a kiss in the middle of a natural shower would make the world stop. Somehow Cameo figured a kiss from Sonny would always make time stand still. Sonny didn't have to think about it. He was already drowning in love and he sure enough didn't like the feeling. When he got to Austin, he was going to call Felicia the first day and make a dinner date with her.

Chapter Nine

From the outside the Strawberry Moon looked dark and closed. But on the inside, back in the kitchen, Cameo whipped eggs in a bowl while Sonny pulled a table from the dining area into the middle of the kitchen floor. He dragged in two chairs next. Then he took two crockery plates from the dish drainer and began to set the table for dinner for two.

"You sure you know how to cook? I'm starving," he peered over her shoulder.

"No, I never made an omelet before. But once upon a time in my castle, that would be complete with a turret and maids by the dozen, I watched the cook make one and I think I can remember how it was done. You just set the table and watch those magnificent biscuits I took from a paper tube. Those are your jobs," she said, her voice carrying more authority than she'd earned in the kitchen. Red said once that he never let her near a stove. She could turn eggs into Dupont rubber in five minutes and she could set the house on fire trying to boil water for a pitcher of tea. Even though her cooking skills did leave something to be desired, she wasn't that bad. What could go wrong with a simple omelet? She'd watched that good looking young man make them at the Opryland Hotel in Nashville. He poured some eggs in the skillet, shook it around a few times, flipped the mixture up in the air, caught it back in the skillet, added all the fillings she'd chosen, and doubled it over on itself. Nothing to it. She had a whole grill in front of her so she'd do fine. It was a simple procedure if she didn't try to toss it in the air for effect.

She set the bowl containing two dozen eggs aside and picked up a whole onion. She'd watched Sonny chop onions lots of times. Half it, place the flat side on the cutting board, slice, being careful to keep the pieces all together, then turn it and begin the second row of slicing. Perfectly diced onions should appear on the board.

The first part was easy. The second step was the stinker. The first cut sent the onion skittering across the floor like a mouse hunting a hidey hole. It exploded when it hit the tile, sending pieces of onion from one end of the kitchen to the other.

"Here, I can do that," he said. "Give me that bell pepper and the ham slice too. I'll get them ready while you make the eggs, then we'll put this on top and flip it."

"Thank you," she said, sidestepping the onions and picking up the eggs to give them a few more turns with the whisk. They'd sweep up the onions later.

A drop of water on the grill danced and sizzled until it evaporated. She poured the eggs out and watched as they spread out over half the hot surface area. Her eyes widened in surprise. She'd expected them to bubble up like they did in the cast iron skillet when the young man made omelets. At the rate they were running over the grill, she'd need to get the scoop shovel from out back to turn them over.

"Looks like we won't be hungry," he chuckled. "How many did you whip up?"

"Whatever was in two boxes in the refrigerator." A drizzle ran out over the grill and onto the floor. She grabbed a wide spatula and pushed the remainder back onto the griddle.

"Two dozen. Four would have been plenty," he said.

"So who died and made you the master chef of this place?" She asked.

"No one, but I do know how to make omelets," he said. "Here, let's scrape this mess off and start all over. I'll make the omelets. You set the table and watch the biscuits."

She handed him the spatula, set her jaw in a tight little line, and cleaned the slimy egg from the side of the grill and the floor. He opened the refrigerator and took out the last container of eggs, finding only four left. He cracked them into the bowl and, using the whisk, whipped them until they were frothy, then poured them on the grill. Just like the previous attempt, they spread out like a big, flat, oversized pancake.

"I should've used a skillet," he mumbled.

"Right," she nodded, her stomach doing everything except whistling Dixie.

He tried to flip the eggs with the wide spatula only to have them turn into nothing more than scrambled eggs with a dark brown bottom. The grill was hot enough to fry hamburgers; too hot by far to make a nice fluffy omelet.

"Little problem there, Tonto?" She taunted.

"No omelets for the princess who lives in the castle tonight, Kemosabe," he folded his arms over his chest.

"Well, rake it off in the trash and let's go to town. Subway ought to still be open," she said.

"No, ma'am. I promised the princess supper at home tonight and we will have it. Throw me four of those burger patties in the icebox. We will have the delicacy known as Strawberry Moon's famous grilled onion burgers," he said.

She produced the meat patties. He poured onions on the grill and added the green peppers as an afterthought. She was so busy watching him make what she figured would be another mess that she forgot about the biscuits until smoke began to pour from the oven.

"Oh, my Lord," she began to beat the smoke with a dish towel. "Do something Sonny."

He opened the oven door to a blast of smoke that set off the alarm screwed firmly to the ceiling right in the middle of the room. He shut his eyes and reached inside blindly, a towel in his hands, to bring out a pan of blackened biscuits. The smoke alarm screamed non stop, smoke filled the kitchen and burned their eyes, and the burgers sizzled as the onions and peppers burned to a crisp around them.

Cameo threw open the back door and rushed out, sucking up lungs full of the night air. Sonny joined her, coughing and sputtering. Then he remembered the burgers burning on the grill and rushed back in the hazy room to turn off the flame from under them. By the time he got back out into the fresh night air, sirens could be heard in the distance. Cameo looked at Sonny. Surely the fire truck wasn't coming to the Moon, not over a pan of burned biscuits.

"How did they know so quickly?" He asked.

She shrugged. The sirens were louder and louder until the red truck pulled right into the parking lot. Wally jumped out of the passenger's seat and literally ran over to them.

"Ya'll alright? Bring the hose over here. Looks like a kitchen fire," he yelled to the driver.

"No!" Cameo screamed. "No, it's just smoke. We burned a pan of biscuits and it smoked. There's no fire. Just smoke."

"You sure?" Wally asked.

"How did you get here so fast?" Sonny asked.

"Millie was on her way back from Ardmore. Saw smoke and Cameo come running out the back door. Called me on the cell phone. I was at a fireman's meeting down at the station. We jumped in the truck and come right on," Wally said.

"Well, we do appreciate it, man, but as you can see, the smoke is already going away," Sonny told him.

"That's what we're here for. Just glad ya'll didn't burn down the cafe. April would've been madder'n a coyote with a muzzle at a chicken convention if you burned down her place. Turn off that fire alarm. Guess the batteries are working alright," Wally laughed at his own joke.

"Now what do we do?" Cameo asked when the tail lights of the fire truck disappeared up the highway.

"Clean up the mess and fix that alarm before it does permanent damage to my ears," Sonny said.

"Doesn't look like we ruined anything," Cameo held

the dining room chair for Sonny to climb onto the table and reach up to pull the plastic alarm down.

He fiddled with it for several minutes before he finally found the reset button, then put it back. When he stepped off the table back onto the red vinyl covered chair he slipped and began to fall. Instinctively Cameo reached out and caught him. It was as if the whole accident happened in slow motion. He slipped. She opened her arms and gathered him into them, and they wobbled for a few minutes before they both slid down onto the kitchen floor.

He looked deeply into the prettiest green eyes he'd ever seen, searching, seeking for the person that Cameo Johnson really was. She gazed into eyes as blue as a summer sky, knowing she could get lost inside them and live forever quite happily. Sonny leaned forward and suddenly his mouth was on hers, his arms around her, drawing her into his embrace.

"Guess we're even," she said when they finally drew apart, embarrassed that she'd let this happen again. High color filled her cheeks and burned her neck. She was thirty years old. She'd kissed and been kissed. So why did the touch of a mere drifter's lips on hers cause her to turn into mush and say the most stupid things in the world?

"Even?" He frowned.

"You caught me and kept me from breaking my neck at the Falls this morning. Remember I fell down the stairs and you caught me? Now I caught you as you were falling. We are even," she said, all in a rush to cover her own insecurities and hating herself for them.

"I see. Well, Miss Even Steven Princess, let's clean up this mess and decide just what we are going to do for supper. It appears omelets are out of the question. And if we get caught with those biscuits we'll be arrested for having concealed weapons on the premises. Do you have a license to carry a deadly weapon like those? If you could've loaded them into a Civil War cannon, they might have turned the tides on the war and the South might have won," he said, trying to cover his feelings with humor.

Cameo picked up the biscuit pan with a pot holder and dumped the black lumps into the trash can. Sonny followed her lead and scooped his onions, peppers, and cremated burgers into the trash with them.

"We'll take some cheese from the 'fridge and some bread. We shall have my famous grilled cheese sandwiches, done in a skillet," she said. Fifteen minutes later they locked the back door of the Moon and carrying their stolen horde to the trailer, leaving nothing behind but the faintest smell of smoke and a million unanswered questions.

"Go sit on the sofa and watch a movie," she told him when they'd unloaded their cafe stash on the bar. "I promise I do know how to make sandwiches. They are my specialty. You should see what I can do with peanut butter and jelly, and my bologna and American cheese are to die for."

"But those don't involve a hot stove," Sonny protested.

"To the sofa. To the living room where the man belongs," she ordered with a nervous giggle. "How many grilled cheese can you eat, Tonto?"

"One," he said seriously. "One if it turns out like your omelet."

"No more negative auras," she threw her hands

around in circles as if cleansing the room from any and all bad thoughts. "Now the air is free from ugly thoughts. I shall make three for you and you will eat them all and, what's more, you shall enjoy them."

"You looked just like Phoebe on *Friends*," he said.

"My favorite sitcom. Love Phoebe. She's so free and honest. I will make supper for you and you'll like it," she said from the kitchen where he noticed she was plugging in an electric skillet. At least that was better than turning on the oven.

Yeah, right, he thought as he shoved a movie into the VCR, surprised that April would have something like *Lethal Weapon* in her house. Either she had never watched it or else that's why she was in Mexico ... doing penance for listening to such language. He smiled as he remembered the part of the movie where Mel Gibson got addicted to dog biscuits. Didn't sound too bad right then when he thought of Cameo cooking. He wondered again where she had come from and who she really was. Her vocabulary didn't fit in with the waitress costume. The fact she couldn't even cook canned biscuits didn't go with the poor little southern girl from the sticks façade. Nothing fit and nothing was right.

He sniffed the air several times and strained his ears above the noise of the movie several times. But nothing was burning. The fire alarm didn't howl and the only sound he could hear was Cameo humming a Travis Tritt tune as she worked. He listened more intently and recognized the tune as "Don't Give Your Heart to a Rambler." Maybe she was thinking about him as she hummed since she viewed him as a rambler or a drifter. He thought about the words to the song. Travis said not to give your heart to a rambler. Sonny hoped Cameo was about to give her heart to a rambler, even if it was in the cards that he break it. A Porsche and a horse were riding on the wager, and she'd get over the heartache.

"Here we go," she set a wooden TV tray in front of him and placed a tall glass of iced tea off to one side. The next trip from the kitchen brought a platter filled with three grilled cheese sandwiches, browned perfectly even, potato chips on one side, pickles on the other. "I found a half gallon of Rocky Road ice cream in the freezer so we have dessert," she said, disappearing back into the kitchen to bring her own food to the living room.

Scratch the idea that she wasn't a poor southern waitress. She could at least cook grilled cheese sandwiches, he thought as he picked up one of the hot sandwiches and bit into the melted cheese inside. Fire filled his mouth as he tried to chew faster and faster to get away from the heat of the cheese and the shooting flames of pepper sauce.

"Got a problem there?" She asked, nibbling at one of her two sandwiches. "I forgot to tell you that my famous grilled cheese sandwiches have a dash of Louisiana hot sauce on them. That's why you've got potato chips and pickles. They take the fire out of your mouth. First bite is always the killer. After that, you'll like them. And remember, we'll chase it with ice cream."

"Ice cream will be wonderful, but I may burn up before I can get it to my mouth," he mumbled.

"Don't whine," she snapped. "It beats your burgers with onions and peppers."

"It sure beats that unholy concoction you tried to pass off for an omelet," he countered.

"Suppose neither of us are just wonderful in the kitchen are we?" She grinned and his heart melted as much as the cheese between the toasted bread.

"Hey, Princess, I've got three weeks' paychecks that say I'm damn good in the kitchen. If the spoiled little princesses stays out of my kitchen, I do just fine. Just ask any one of those kids bound for Falls Creek where they get saved, sanctified, and dehorned all in a week," he retorted.

She giggled.

"What's so funny?" He demanded.

"Just that three weeks ago you didn't know jack squat from Shinola in the kitchen and now you are a professional chef? Maybe you ought to go with those kids for a week to the church camp. Who knows? Maybe it would be a good place to hide from the mob or whoever it is they're protecting you from," she said.

"And three weeks ago you didn't know anything about waitress work either or I'll eat my dirty sneakers for breakfast," he said.

"Fast learners, aren't we?" She filled her mouth with more sandwich and followed it with a long gulp of tea. So she'd gotten carried away with the pepper sauce—she'd never admit it.

Chapter Ten

W here had the month gone? Cameo's eyebrows knit together above her glasses. Somehow the time that was supposed to have crept by like some homeless old man with no place to go and forever to get there had sped past faster than gossip. She expertly mopped the floor for the last time. Tomorrow she'd say good-bye to Sonny and go to Austin. Where he went would be his own business, but he'd be taking a good sized chunk of her heart with him. Hopefully hearts had the ability to grow back or else sear over after a spell and she would get over the rambler she'd fallen for in spite of her desperate attempts to keep it from happening.

Sonny dumped the old grease in the right disposal container, wiped down all the counter tops in the kitchen, and made sure it was spotless. It was the least he could do for April since he'd be long gone on Monday morning. He wouldn't want to face a nasty kitchen and five church vans loaded with kids on the same day. He checked everything one more time and went up front to help Cameo finish her chores. She and Joyce would go back to Dallas to their secretary pool. He wondered if Cameo was listed in the telephone book, should he ever have a weak moment and want to call her. He hoped not. A clean break was more important. Besides, if he did call she would not jump up and down with joy at the sound of his voice.

That's the truth, he thought. After tomorrow she'd probably shoot him on sight, throw his sorry old carcass in the Red River and not even suffer a second's worth of guilt. But he'd come too far to back down now. He patted the pocket of his jeans where the little velvet box waited, and slipped the micro-recorder in the other pocket. He was on the brink of proving his father and Red Marshall dead wrong and that brought a smile to his handsome face. What he was about to do to Cameo wiped it off.

"All finished," she said. "You sure took your sweet time getting the kitchen done. Tonto must not like to mop."

"No, this Indian doesn't like to mop. But he would have helped like he's done every night, except he wanted to leave the kitchen spotless for the owners. Wouldn't want them thinking we hadn't earned our money, now would we, Princess?" He said. "Shall we turn out the lights and take a final walk to the double wide mansion one more time?"

"I guess so," she mumbled. One long last look and they flipped the switch.

Darkness surrounded them as they walked home like they'd done every night for a month. Sonny reached across and took her hand in his, liking the way it fit so naturally there. "Shall we have one more water fight before we go on to the mysterious future?" He asked when they reached the porch.

"No, this princess is too tired to chase wild Indians with wicked water hoses." She sat down on the top porch step.

Without letting go of her hand, he joined her. "It's been a good month, Cameo. I don't know when I've ever worked so hard, lived on so little, or enjoyed it so much. All but that twin sized bed with the Barbie sheets. I won't miss that one bit. The next place I go will have a king sized bed."

"Not for fifty bucks a week it won't. You'll be lucky to get a pink room with a bathroom of your own and laundry privileges for that amount," she told him.

"Cameo, I know we said no past and no future. Just today. I've loved living with that, but I've got a bit of a problem," he rubbed the inside of her thumb.

She shivered from the sensation it evoked. "Oh, do I need to write a note to the WP program and tell them you've been a good boy and learned a new trade?"

"No, nothing that simple," he said, sincere desperation in his voice.

"Then if it's not got anything to do with the past or the future and only this minute, then spit it out, Tonto," she squeezed his hand.

He slyly reached into his pocket and flipped a little switch. "I'm afraid I've fallen in love with you, Cameo. Didn't mean to. Fought it with all I had. But it's happened. It's not just sharing time but it's sharing hearts. I'm hoping I haven't read the signs all wrong all month and you feel the same about me. Now not knowing the past or the future. With just what we know, can you trust me enough to marry me?"

"Did I just hear you right? Did you propose to me?" She asked incredulously.

"I did. I'm asking you to be my wife. Tomorrow morning we can discuss the past. We can even talk about the future. But tonight under these stars I'm declaring my love for you. I'm telling you I want to spend the rest of my life with you. I'm asking you to marry me without asking any questions." He held his breath as he waited.

Red Marshall would have a cardiac arrest. Joyce would hyperventilate. She just had a proposal from a man who had no idea about her material worth or that she was heir to half an oil corporation so rich it would make a sheik's eyes pop out.

She couldn't do it. She could not marry a drifter who in all likelihood was in the witness protection program. A man with a tattoo on his arm and whose only mode of transportation was a Harley.

But she loved him. Really loved him.

She couldn't not be honest.

"Yes, I will marry you," she said speaking from her heart instead of her mind.

He pushed the button on the micro-recorder, turning the machine off. He had the proof. He gathered her into his arms and kissed her passionately, "You've made me the happiest man in the whole world. I'll tell you the whole truth tomorrow morning, but let's live just one more night in the glory of the present and not go into the past."

"I love you too," Cameo mumbled, liking the way

their hearts beat in unison. Tomorrow she'd own up to
her own secrets too. But tonight was theirs.

"Wait a minute," he said pulling back from her. "It's
not nearly what you deserve and I hope its the right
size." He dug deep into his pocket and brought out the
velvet box, opening it for her.

"How did you do that?" She looked at the tiny diamond sparkling in the moon light. "When did you have
time?"

He removed the ring from the box and put it on her
finger. It fit perfectly. "Remember when I volunteered
to run into town to the grocery store a few days ago, the
day we ran out of lettuce? I picked it up then. It's not as
big as you deserve but then if I bought one as big as the
love I have for you, you'd have to push it around in a
wheel barrow."

"It's perfect," she held it up to catch what light there
was. A simple little round diamond on a gold band. She
wrapped her arms around him and covered his face
with kisses. Never had Ivy Marshall been so happy.

It had cost him half of the money he'd made that
month and at that was a good investment, he'd figured
when he hurried into the jewelry store on the south side
of Main Street and purchased it. He had proof that he'd
caught a woman, a waitress. He had pay stubs to prove
he'd worked twelve hours a day for a month. He'd slept
on a twin sized bed in a room with only kiddie movies
to watch. So why did he feel like the south end of a
north bound donkey?

"I can't tell you . . ." he whispered into her hair.

"I know," she put her fingers on his lips to quiet him.
"We'll talk tomorrow, but right now I'm going to either
fall asleep in your arms right here or else you're going

to have to let me go inside and get some sleep. Tomorrow is Sunday. We'll have all day to talk, and I'm thinking it might take all day to cover what we're going to have to say. Then we will need to discuss the other end . . . the future," she said.

"The F-word," he chuckled. "That's what my buddies say when a woman says anything about the future. It means there's a commitment. A relationship and they run from that faster than they would a Texas rattlesnake."

"Well, we'll have to think about that F-word," she pulled his face toward hers for one more kiss. One more of those passionate kisses to fill her insides with mush. One more to convince her she wasn't certifiably goofy for just getting engaged to Sonny Johnson, a man on the run, a fry cook. But he made her so blasted happy and she would marry him.

He carried her into the house and right up to her bedroom door. "I love you, Cameo," he said one more time. He kissed her lightly on the end of her nose. "Goodnight darling. Until tomorrow." He left her standing in front of the door as he blew kisses all the way across the living room floor.

Inside the bedroom, she gently closed the door and slid down the backside. What in the world had she just done? Consented to marry Sonny? It was a dream. No, it was a nightmare. She pinched her bare arm and it hurt like a big dog. It wasn't a dream.

Reality hit her in the gut like a freight train slamming into a two hole outhouse. She couldn't do it. No, she could not. She lifted her finger and gazed at the diamond engagement ring. Much, much smaller than the diamond her father had given her for her sixteenth birthday. She shook her head. She shouldn't compare. In respect to what Red Marshall was worth and what Sonny Johnson was worth, it was twice as big. What was the matter with her, anyway? She wasn't materialistic. She didn't care if her husband gave her a plain gold band just like her mother had worn.

At midnight she was still fighting with herself, still leaning against the door. At one o'clock, she'd decided she would marry him, no matter if it did create a storm that would make a hurricane look like a summer breeze. They'd find a place for Sonny in the corporation. He caught on fast. He could start at the bottom and work his way up. Anyone could learn to be a roustabout. At two o'clock she'd changed her mind, knowing in six months he'd be miserable. He was a man's man, not one who'd be content with his wife bringing the majority of the income. That's what she loved about him. His complete and total honesty . . . at least for today. If he wouldn't discuss the past and wouldn't discuss the future, at least he was honest today. At four o'clock she had her duffel bag packed. At five she looked in the yellow pages to call a cab. None were listed for Davis so she phoned the police station and asked if there were any that might not be listed. The lady dispatcher told her that there were no cabs in Davis.

"But I've got to get to Dallas and I need to leave in an hour," Cameo panicked. She had to be gone before he awoke. She couldn't face him and tell him she'd changed her mind. There was too much chemistry. She'd capitulate the minute he kissed her.

"Honey, the only thing I know to tell you is that there is a limousine service if you want to spend that much money. Let me give you the number. You might call them," the lady said.

An hour later a big white limousine pulled up in the parking lot of the Strawberry Moon. Cameo took the time to put a note on the desk in her bedroom to Joyce telling her that she'd gone on to Dallas early and would see her in Austin tomorrow morning. Board meeting was set to start at nine o'clock. They had a lot of catching up to do so they'd have lunch and Joyce could tell her all about the Mexican romance with the Davis businessman. Then she tucked another note into the blender. Sonny would find it when he awoke and made his smoothie for breakfast. It simply said:

I'm so sorry, but I can't do this, Sonny. You don't know who I am or what I am. It would never work between us, so I'd rather end it before it begins, because to start and then fail would tear my soul apart. I do love you. Please know that. Cameo.

She threw her bag into the back of the limousine and told the driver to take her to the DFW airport. One last look at the cafe, the trailer, the motorcycle sitting beside Joyce's Lexus—she almost walked right back into the trailer and forgot about leaving. But she couldn't. She simply could not marry a rambler that she knew nothing about. She curled up on the broad back seat and cried herself to sleep.

Sonny fought his own battles all night long. At midnight he crept up the hallway to her bedroom door, sat down with his back against it and told himself he was the biggest jerk ever to walk upon the face of the earth. He'd knock on the door, awaken his new fiancée from her sleep and tell her the truth, forfeit his horse and sports car. Nothing was worth hurting a woman like he was about to do when he left her.

Call it cowardice. He couldn't tell her he really did love her but he'd duped her. He couldn't marry Cameo. She'd be lost in his world of business suits and trips to Europe. She'd grow to hate him in six months. She could never trust him when she found out about the wager. Better to end it now. He raised his hand to knock on the door, but he couldn't do it.

He'd leave her a note and escape back into his world with only half a heart. He went back to his pink room and spent the rest of the night composing notes and destroying them. At five o'clock he stretched out on the bed and fell into a fitful exhausted sleep. At six thirty he awoke, packed his few belongings in a duffel bag, hurriedly wrote a note and left it in the refrigerator beside her yogurt container. It read:

Cameo, please forgive me. I can't do this. I simply can not take you into my world where you would never fit in. I do love you, but love wouldn't hold together a marriage between two people as different as we are in the real world. The past haunts us. The future scares us. The present was beautiful. I wish we could have stayed there. Sonny.

Her bedroom door was still closed when he slipped out the front door, crammed his bag into the trunk of the Harley, and pushed it all the way out to the highway. Before he left he looked around one more time. The Strawberry Moon where he'd made the best onion burgers in the whole south of Oklahoma. The double wide trailer and the Lexus still parked under the carport. It had been an experience alright. He fired up the cycle and headed south toward Love Field, where he'd catch the next plane out of Dallas going to Austin. At the top of the mountain he pulled off at the scenic look out, put his quarter in the telescope machine, and used up every second of the allotted time, staring at the falls through it, scarcely blinking. The place where he finally admitted to himself one week ago that he was in love with Cameo Johnson. When the quarter's worth of time finished, he pulled a tiny tape from his pocket and dropped it in the trash can beside the telescope.

Chapter Eleven

Emerald green silk suit with a celery green shirt. Very tasteful herringbone gold bracelet and matching small hoop earrings. No necklace. Tiny, diamond engagement ring relegated to the safe behind the picture above the foyer table. Make-up perfect. Hair pulled back in a chaste chignon. Simple pumps of dark green kidskin leather. Glasses thrown on the foyer table. Contact lenses in. Cameo Johnson was gone. Ivy Marshall was ready for her first day of work in the new company.

The elevator up to the top floor of the DH Enterprise building squeaked just slightly. Cameo listened intently and jumped only slightly when the door bell buzzed. She threw it open to find Joyce, a grin on her face and two cups of Starbuck's coffee in her hands.

"You are a sight for sore eyes," Ivy grabbed Joyce in a hug.

"Who? Me or Mr. Starbuck?" She asked.

"Both," Ivy took one of the disposable cups from her hand and sipped the strong black liquid. "Wonderful. We've got about ten minutes. Tell me everything you can cram into it."

"You go first. I found your note on the desk. April was tickled pink with the rent money from your boarder. The Moon was in wonderful shape. Guess I owe you two weeks in December. Can you make it the first of December, though? Like from the first to the fifteenth?" April's grin was absolutely infectious.

"Why? So you can spend Christmas week doing waitress work at the Moon so your sister can go off to Mexico again?" Ivy asked.

"No, because I'm giving notice. Formally later on today. Have it all written up. Remember the smothering businessman? The one from Davis? Well, about two nights ago I came up for air when he was off with my brother-in-law doing last minute touches on the house we built. Found out I didn't like it. He proposed. I accepted. But I've got this commitment to you for those weeks, so we're planning a Christmas wedding. I'll be moving to Davis," Joyce said.

Ivy was too stunned to speak.

"Say something. Tell me I'm crazy to consider such a thing. Tell me I'll never be happy in that little town," Joyce said nervously.

"I can't speak," Ivy said. "I could never tell you those things anyway. Davis is wonderful. Warm. Friendly. Hospitable. I might go back there myself if . . ." she let her voice trail off.

"Well, I'll be hung from the nearest mesquite tree," Joyce laughed. "You got bit by the small town bug.

Don't worry, darlin', you can come and visit with me and Cyrus anytime you want to. You'll always have a room in that big old rambling two story house he's got outside of town."

"Cyrus?" Ivy wrinkled her nose.

"Named after his great-grandfather," Joyce said with a giggle. "Time to go. Can't be late for the first board meeting. Let's go meet the lions and show them the lioness is the one who brings home the bacon."

Ivy smiled wanly, memories washing over her heart as she thought of the lion she'd left behind. The door right across the hall from hers where the other vice president had a suite of rooms was still closed. Ivy frowned at it. The rich Will Dalhart. Her only neighbor. One she didn't care to ever know past the third floor of the business.

"You can get married before Christmas if you want to. I won the wager, but I don't want the prizes," she said on the way down to the second floor where the board room was already set up for the first meeting.

"You serious?" Joyce could scarcely believe her ears.

"Yes, I am. I'm going to miss you horribly, and I'll never be able to replace you, but go where your heart is. Don't ever let anyone tell you not to listen to it," Ivy said.

"Sounds like you've got a couple of stories to tell of your own," Joyce said. "I'll talk to Cyrus. Maybe we'll think about a late fall wedding after all. Six weeks notice good enough?"

"Good enough," Ivy said.

"Will you come to Davis and be my maid of honor?"

"Thought you'd never ask. But only if you don't ask

that horrid Millie to be a bride's maid," Ivy smiled, but it didn't reach her eyes.

"I'd elope first. She's a first rate witch, isn't she? Glad you got to know her. Now any woman you ever meet will be a saint compared to that," Joyce said.

The doors opened and they crossed a thickly carpeted hallway to double doors opening into a room that even smelled new. The mahogany table from the old conference room in Dallas had been moved, but the chairs had evidently come from Houston because Ivy had never seen them before. The water pitchers she recognized. The glasses she didn't. A folder had already been placed before each of the twelve chairs. A table with doughnuts, bagels, and fresh fruit was set up under the expansive windows where Texas sunlight poured into the room.

"Time to play ball. This part belongs to you. I'm going to the third floor to my new-for-six-weeks office. Go get 'em, Ivy. Don't let any of those old lions intimidate you," Joyce winked.

Ivy slowly touched each chair, beginning at the end closest to the door where the folder had Will Dalhart's name on it. She recognized half the names; the other half had merged in with Houston. At least she wouldn't be completely in the dark. At the other end of the table was her folder with her name, Ivy Marshall. She paused for a second. That's who she really was. Ivy Marshall. Not Cameo Johnson. That was part of the history of the past now. Ivy was the present and the future.

People began to pour in. Those she knew introducing her to the three piece suits she didn't. They seemed an amiable group, standing around the refreshment table, talking of sports, fishing, the newest off shore drilling, the price of a barrel of oil, how much the recent wars had effected the business, whose grandfather had drilled that gusher over in east Texas that got the whole business started. Ivy fit right in and no one seemed to even notice that she wasn't wearing pants with her expensive suit.

"Well, would you look here. The prodigal princess finally comes home," Red's presence filled the double doors. He might be a medium sized man, but a force preceded him into every room.

She met him in the middle of the room with a big hug. "I missed you, Daddy."

"And you won the wager. So I'd guess you didn't miss me too badly," he laughed. "Call the Caddy company and tell them what you want. I can't believe you stayed on like that. Guess you got my blood after all."

"I won the wager. That's enough. I don't want or need a new Caddy," she smiled. "Don't think I could ever look at it without remembering the past month."

"And all the hard work?" Red asked.

"The hardest work and most difficult decisions I've ever done or made," she said honestly.

"Well, that makes my check book laugh out loud," he said. "Hey, ya'll meet my daughter. She's the smartest, hardest working girl on the block and she'll keep you on your toes and the IRS out of your face."

Ivy smiled. "Maybe not the smartest or the hardest working, but I'll guarantee you that the business end of this corporation will be run honestly and without error."

"That's what we want," one man nodded. "You keep

us in the black and the IRS at bay and Will can keep the wells bringing in black gold."

"Met Will yet?" Red asked mischievously. "Run into him in the hall or ride in the elevator with him?"

"No. He can stay on his side of the hall and I'll be sure to stay on mine. Business and pleasure don't mix, and you know that," she wiggled a finger at Red. Her nails were hopelessly short, but they'd grow back. Mop water and dish towels didn't go with long, lovely red nails. Nor did biting them half the night on Saturday while she fought a legion of demons.

"Where's my son?" John Dalhart's big booming voice filled the room from the double doors.

"He's not as prompt as my daughter," Red goaded him. "Guess he had a rough weekend and isn't coming down until the last minute."

"Maybe Will is having breakfast in his apartment," Ivy said in defense of the man she dreaded meeting.

Three piece tailored suit. Handmade eel cowboy boots. A bolo tie with a slide in the shape of Texas, encrusted in diamonds. Hair feathered back in a perfect cut. Clean shaven. The journal hidden in the safe behind the oil painting of an oil wooden derrick right above the foyer table. Temporary tattoo removed. Sonny Johnson was dead. Will Dalhart was ready for work.

He waited until eight forty five and picked up the phone.

"Hello," a sleepy voice greeted him.

"Felicia, this is Will. I'm in Austin with the new corporation. How about dinner tonight?" He asked.

"Love to. Got some great news to share with you, darlin'. Been forever since I've had a hug from you. You flying down here or want me to come there?" She said without an ounce of enthusiasm.

"It'll be a big day. I'll send the company plane for you. The limo will pick you up and bring you to the restaurant. Eight thirty dinner?" He tapped the corner of the picture as he talked.

"Sounds good to me. Don't send the company plane, though. Daddy bought me my own for my birthday, plus a full time pilot. That's what the idea of grand-children does to a man his age. Don't pick a seafood restaurant. Remember I hate it. Get us reservations at a good steak house," she said. "Black tie?"

"No, just a nice place," he said. "See you at eight thirty then?"

"Looking forward to it, Will. Have a good first day at the office," she laughed. "I'm glad Daddy never made me work."

"Pretty as you are, darlin', it would be a shame for you to work," he teased but the mood didn't reach his heart.

"Flattery will get you everywhere," she said. "Good-bye, Will."

He slid the cordless phone into place and opened the door out into the hallway. There was Ivy Marshall's door right across from his. All it needed was a shiny gold name plate to be more offensive. They'd have to work together every single day. Him in her office more than she'd be in his. Red had said when the merger was still in the first stages that his daughter was a business barracuda. That's exactly what he did not want or need.

A woman to tell him he couldn't drill because it wasn't feasible.

He slapped the button on the elevator and waited impatiently. They'd all be in the conference room by now. Eating doughnuts and bagels. Telling stories. Swapping weekend tales of fishing and sports. How on earth did a woman intend to fit into that? He could see hiring a good accountant, one that the IRS respected as Red had bragged, but to make her the vice president of the company? That was a far reach. Not that he had a problem working with women. Hadn't he just proved that this past month? No ma'am. It was hiring one just because she was Red's daughter that galled him. To have to share the vice president slot instead of having the president's chair all to himself didn't set too well with Will Dalhart as the elevator doors opened and he paused a moment before entering the big, open doors into the first Monday morning meeting of the new oil enterprise.

Leaving the men to a conversation about oil in Alaska, Ivy pulled out her chair and opened her folder. Rows of figures where her brain was right at home. Projections for the first year. A brief profile of everyone employed in the corporation. She flipped open to hers to see a picture taken last year and a biography stating where she'd gotten her bachelor's degree, her master's, and her doctorate, plus a list of all her accomplishments. Looked pretty impressive, but it didn't have the most important job she'd ever done . . . waitress at the Strawberry Moon cafe in Davis, Oklahoma.

"And here he is. Time to line up, boys, and get to work," John said.

She felt the mood of the room change to a more serious aura as everyone took their seats and poured themselves glasses of water. The meeting would begin. She frantically flipped through the pages in search of Will Dalhart. Where had he been educated? What were his credentials? What did he look like?

"I'd like to introduce my son, Will Dalhart," John said from the other end of the table. "There's a couple of pages in the folders before you stating all the important things about him. But as his father and the one who's handing the reins over to him today just before I go back to Houston and raise horses in my retirement, I'm telling you that I trust him to run this business. Red Marshall will be acting president, but he's retiring in all but name just like I am. Now everyone make my son welcome and he'll make you money."

A round of applause sounded as Ivy continued to thumb through the book in search of Will's picture.

"And I'd like to introduce my daughter, Ivy Marshall," Red said from behind her chair. Like John said, I'm just acting president. These two are running the business soon as I can get out of here and get my jeans and work boots on in Dallas. Will, I'm sure, will make money and raise the stock value, but Ivy, the other vice president, is going to make sure that money is well protected and safe. Now Ivy, you and Will stand up so everyone can see their new bosses."

She closed the folder and pushed her chair back. When she looked up, it was into the bluest eyes in all of Texas and southern Oklahoma. Straight into Sonny Johnson's eyes.

Will's mouth went dry. If that wasn't Cameo Johnson at the end of the table, minus the glasses, he'd give his first year's paycheck to the first street bum he bumped into.

Ivy thanked everyone in an only slightly squeaky voice. She managed about half of her prepared speech and hoped she didn't sound too much like a fifth grader giving her first talk in front of a classroom. When she sat down, anger boiled up from the bottom of her expensive shoes.

Will sucked his jaws in and found enough moisture to at least deliver the majority of his speech, thanking his father and Red for their trust. He hoped he didn't sound too much like a political candidate for the job of governor of the state of Texas.

"And now if you would excuse me and Miss Ivy Marshall. We need to have a meeting in my office," he said, gathering up the folder and starting toward the door.

Both fathers and Ivy followed him.

A sharp machete couldn't have cut its way through the thick tension filling the elevator on the way down to the second floor. John and Red were grinning. Steam boiled out of Ivy's ears. Will tapped his foot. Wall to wall mirrors kept all of them from being able to ignore each other.

It was Cameo alright, right down to her aristocratic nose. The only thing missing was the jeans, tee shirt, and apron—and ugly glasses. His icy gaze was met with one so hot it threatened to set the elevator aflame.

So Sonny Johnson was really Will Dalhart, she used the mirrors to glare right into those blue eyes. Was it all a big joke?

"Okay, you two sit down and let me talk first," Red said when they were inside Will's office was an exact replica of Ivy's. Same view. Same new, shiny furnishings. Same corner of the building.

Will took his place behind the desk. Ivy sat primly in the chair furthest from him, crossed her legs at the ankle and waited, shooting rounds of .38 Special bullets at his forehead with her continuing glare. She couldn't work with him. Not ever. Not after what had gone on in Davis.

"It all started out right innocent," Red said. "Me and Joyce got to teasing Ivy and goaded her into working in that cafe up there in Davis, Oklahoma for a month. I never thought she'd make it the whole month. Never figured I'd have to ante up for a brand new Cadillac. Then I got the bright notion that John and I could make a wager on the side. Ever since I went down to his horse farm in Houston, I've been trying to purchase one of his horses and he won't sell me the one I want. So we made a deal. If we could goad Will into a similar situation, we'd do a little betting. If Will come home whining, then I got my horse. If Ivy didn't last, John here got his bull. Seems like we both lost, but we've been talking and we're going to sell the other one the livestock anyway. So we didn't win and we didn't lose."

"We never figured that Will would go to work in the Strawberry Moon. We just thought it'd be a hoot if you two met each other and didn't know who the other one was. Guess you won that new sports car and the horse fair and square, son," John said.

"Yes, I did," Will said. "But I'm not collecting on the bet. I proved to you both I can work at anything."

"And you both proved you can work together, so Red and I are out of here to have a bite of lunch and then the company plane is taking us home," John said. "You kids run this like you did that Strawberry Moon, only on a bigger scale. I'll be keeping touch, son," he said as he and Red clamored out the door.

Their raucous laughter could be heard until the elevator doors closed.

"Cameo?" Will asked icily.

"Sonny?" She returned cold for cold.

"Did you find my note?" He asked.

"Did you find mine?" She countered.

"I left you a note on the yogurt inside the refrigerator. The Lexus was still there when I left so I know you found it," he said.

"The motorcycle and Lexus were still there when my limo pulled out of the cafe parking lot. The note I left you was inside the blender," she said.

"And what did it say?" He asked.

"It doesn't matter. I made the right choice in changing my mind. Guess I knew all along you weren't to be trusted. What did yours say?" She bit the inside of her lower lip. It hurt like sin. No, she wasn't having the ultimate nightmare. This was reality.

"Same thing. Now what are we going to do?" He asked.

"We're going to run this business. You keep your end and I'll keep mine. Business and pleasure don't mix anyway. We've just proven that, haven't we?" She said.

"What color Caddy are you getting for your month at the Moon?" He asked.

"That's pleasure, Will Dalhart. It doesn't mix with business, which is the only thing I intend to discuss with you from this day forth. I'll be in my office if you need anything to do with business. Good day to you," she said, stiffening her back and walking out of his office and hopefully out of his life.

Chapter Twelve

"**I** simply can not believe that tale," Joyce said. "Will Dalhart was your vagabond, the man you hired for a fry cook? Please believe me, I didn't know anything about that. I can't believe Red and John Dalhart did that. You should've told him he owed you a full length mink coat and a Caddy, or hired a hit man for them both."

"It's the truth. I did leave him a note in the blender, though. And I'd sure like to have it back if you'd ask April for it. He says he left one in the 'fridge for me and I want that one too," Ivy said.

"I'll call her this morning," Joyce said. "I've already talked to Cyrus. Told him we didn't have to wait until Christmas. He's walking on air. We've decided on the second weekend in September and he's already on the phone booking a two week cruise."

"Congratulations, Joyce. I won't even think about you being gone. Lord, we've been inseparable since kindergarten, but I'm so happy for you. Please don't

148

tell me I have to wear a big, bouffant pink chiffon dress," Ivy winced at the visual picture.

"No, I'm thinking orange. Bright orange," Joyce teased.

Ivy slapped at her across the desk. "I already have an orange tankini I bought at Turner Falls. We wouldn't have to shop for a dress . . ."

"Not on your life, Ivy Marshall! We're having the old timey kind of wedding. Candles everywhere. A reception where the whole town of Davis is invited. Cake as tall as me. And a groom's cake nearly that big. We're thinking of an outdoor wedding and reception at Turner Falls. They're going to shut it down for the weekend to anyone except the wedding guests. I'm hoping everyone in the whole town turns out. I really like those folks up there," Joyce ticked off the plans on her fingers like a four year old counting for the first time.

"Can they do that?" Ivy asked, a grin covering her face as she thought about again seeing the ladies from the grocery store, the young married group from church, and all the rest of the friendly people she'd met in that sleepy little town in southern Oklahoma.

"Sure. It's after Labor Day and basically the tourist trade is finished by then. Of course there's a few die hards who come up for the weekend all winter, but the big part of the trade is over. Cyrus says he'll rent the whole park if he needs to. He's lived there his whole life. I think his grandfather or great-grandfather six times removed or something squatted in a cow pasture and they built the town around him. Anyway, that's what we've got going. And you are going to wear a gorgeous original creation of emerald green silk. Straight as a judge. Slit up to your thigh and cut down low, so low that you'll show off four inches of cleavage," Joyce said.

"Sounds more like a barmaid's dress than a maid of honor's gown," Ivy tried to get into the spirit but she wasn't finished being mad just yet. "I suppose we'd best get to work on something other than wedding plans, though. First off, start a list of who I can interview for your replacement. Then bring me the hard copy reports for the whole month that I've been gone," she typed in commands on the keyboard and spreadsheets appeared on the computer screen while she thought out loud.

"Daddy's gotten things running smoothly I'm sure, but he's like a bull in a China closet when it comes to computers. I want to cross check everything. I don't know who he had working the computer. Sure hope it wasn't him. After that make reservations for us at some steak house in town. I don't care which one. I'm just starving for a rare steak and a bottle of good red wine, and I think celebration is in order with the news you've just sprung on me," Ivy said.

The phone rang and she picked it up, answering, "DH Enterprises."

Joyce waved and disappeared into her adjoining office while Ivy conducted the first business of the new day. She had absolutely no idea where a good steak house was in Austin, Texas. Put her in Dallas and she'd pick up the phone and make reservations at one of more than a dozen that she and Ivy both liked.

She pulled two heavy folders from a file cabinet and looked through the window into Ivy's office. Ivy was still talking on the phone, a frown on her face as if she didn't like what she was hearing. Joyce slipped into the office and put the reports on her desk. Ivy nodded and mouthed, "Thank you," and kept writing fast and furious on a note pad.

Joyce sat down at her own desk and toyed with a list of people she thought would be qualified to replace her. Someone within the firm. Someone who'd worked hard, was educated, and could get along with Ivy. She came up with four names off the top of her head. Four more after ten more minutes of deep thought.

"Now the steak house," she mumbled. She thumbed through the phone book and there were pages of restaurants, some even named such and such steak house. But which one was good? She grabbed the phone and pushed the button to get the door man.

"Marvin here," his deep voice came over the line.

"Marvin, this is Joyce, Miss Ivy Marshall's associate. I need to know the best steak house in town so I can make reservations and we need a company car brought around at eight o'clock," she said.

"Miss Joyce, the steak house I recommend the most is The Steak House. Good atmosphere and the wine selection is wonderful. A bit expensive, but worth it. They've got a lovely menu of seafood available too. Anyway, if you're having steak, ask for a bottle of their *Chateau La Gomerie* wine. It's on the reserved list. And a car . . . let's see. Mr. Will Dalhart has requested that we send the white one to the airport and pick up a companion for him. Will the black one do?" He asked.

"The black one will be fine, Marvin," she said. "Ready at eight, then?"

"Consider it done, ma'am," Marvin said.

Joyce circled The Steak House in the phone book

and immediately called for reservations at eight thirty. She wouldn't mention that Will had plans for the night too—ones that involved a long white limo.

Will showered and changed into a different suit. Same black material, but cut a little different. He slipped his feet into sleek leather cowboy boots and combed his hair back. He'd had a good day. The transfer went as smooth as silk. The same crew he'd had in Houston had transferred to Austin. They'd added the Dallas staff, but the guys already knew each other from the previous month. By the end of the day, Will had committed the new associates' names to memory and everything was running like a well oiled machine.

Everything, that is, except his personal life. He hadn't had to deal with Ivy all day. Not even once. But every morning from now on, he would. They'd have a thirty minute conference where he'd better remember to wear winter weight suits to ward off the chill. How was he supposed to know she was really Ivy Marshall, the oil baroness with a doctorate degree? Yes, he'd looked up everything he could find on her once she left his office. No wonder she could run the Strawberry Moon so efficiently. It was like licking icing off a cake compared to managing a whole oil empire.

The phone rang and he held his breath, hoping Felicia hadn't backed out at the last minute. Of all the things he really needed, it was an evening with an old friend like Felicia. They'd thought about being more than friends one time back in college, but somewhere in the courtship they'd figured out they were more suited to friendship than romance. And that's the way it had been ever since.

"Hello," he answered it on the third ring.

"This is Marvin at the door. The car and your companion await," he said.

"Thank you Marvin. I'm on my way down," he did a little jig as he shut the door behind him. An evening with Felicia where nothing could possibly go wrong. Not like the one when Cameo tried to burn down the hamburger joint. He set his jaw and determined he wouldn't think about her again. Out of sight; out of mind. That kind of thing. It was over. He'd been a different man. She'd been a wholly different woman. What they were and what they really were couldn't be blended.

"Mr. Dalhart," Marvin held the door for him.

"Thank you Marvin, and thanks for the tip on the restaurant also. I'm afraid I'll have to learn my way around Austin. I've been here a few times when we were looking for a building but never very long," he smiled brightly at the doorman.

"My pleasure, Mr. Dalhart. Glad to be of assistance. Call me anytime. I hear a lot of recommendations and complaints both. Wouldn't ever send you to a place that I'd heard wasn't fit to take a dog to," Marvin grinned back.

"Felicia, darlin'," Will slid across the wide seat and planted a kiss on her cheek. "You are a sight for sore eyes."

"Well, you aren't. You've got circles the color of a cow patty under your eyes. Where have you been and what's been going on? I thought you were going to relax for a month."

"Had a change of plans. I worked all month," he said. "But now that everything is back in routine, the circles . . . did you say the color of cow patties? Good Lord, what a thing to say to a man," he chuckled.

"Truth is truth. Don't know that it changes colors for male or female," she said bluntly.

"Well, you look lovely," he said.

"And you lie so well," she laughed. "I'm too fat by ten pounds and at thirty three I don't seem to give a damn. But darlin' I brought the most wonderful news. Look at what Ray gave me last week," she held up her left hand where a diamond only slightly smaller than an ice skating rink sparkled in spite of the darkness. "He's going to make an honest woman of me at Christmas and we're flying off to Italy for a few weeks."

"Felicia, I'm so happy for you," he hugged her tightly.

"And then we are coming home and starting a family. Have to get started soon. My biological clock is ticking loudly and Ray is forty five, you know. I figure about six kids in the next seven years should be enough to keep us busy," she eyed the ring a while longer, then dropped it into her lap.

"Six?" Will exclaimed.

"Or maybe seven if I'm still able to have another one after that. I told you years ago, when I settled down I was having kids. Of all the things I hate about my parents, the one thing I hate most is that they didn't at least give me one sister or brother," she said.

"I've been your brother," he said.

"And a fine one you've been, too, but I want my kids to have bunches, and they will. Ray says we can have as many as I want. Momma says I'll change my mind after the first visit to the labor room. I reminded her that was the reason they made drugs. I'd have six if it killed me just to prove to her I can," she said.

"I'm sure you will, darlin'," he patted her hand. "And congratulations. Can I be the maid of honor?"

"Of course. That was my next question. Ray's sister is standing up with him. We're having a small wedding. Only six or seven hundred guests at the ranch. Momma is already talking flowers and caterers. I want you to be my attendant. Who else would I have?" she asked.

"Please don't tell me I have to wear a pink frothy dress," he intoned.

"I was thinking more a Hawaiian print shirt and Bermuda shorts. I told Momma we'd have a beach wedding theme and she almost died. Said I was her only daughter, only child matter of fact, and she was having the wedding of her dreams. So I think you'll be wearing a formal tux with tails. Sorry to disappoint you," she smiled.

"I suppose I'll survive. I have lived through worse this past month," he intoned dramatically.

"Want to talk about it?" She asked.

"No, I wouldn't spoil this evening for you for the whole world. Looks like we're here. I understand this joint makes the best steak in the whole great state of Texas," he held the door for her.

"If it's better than Daddy's grilled ribeyes, then I'll put a hundred dollar tip on the table," she said, taking his hand and sliding out. Taller than Will by at least three inches, she wore a simple off the shoulder black dress and spike heels. Her gigantic engagement ring was the only jewelry she wore that night.

They were seated at a secluded table in a corner and

the waiter brought menus. Felicia wasted no time flipping hers open and was about to order an appetizer of breaded Brie when she noticed Will's jaw knotting up in pure anger. At first she thought perhaps he had the onset of a violent headache, but then she recognized the expression for what it really was. She'd seen it often in the past when he was so mad he could kill a grizzly bear with his scowl.

"What on earth has happened?" She asked.

He didn't say a word, just literally glared at two women being escorted to the table right next to theirs.

"Why that's Ivy Marshall," Felicia said. "I met her at a party in Dallas last fall. Remember I told you about it? Right before ya'll started talking about this big merger thing with your companies. She's smart as Einstein. She'll be a fine asset to your company, but you probably already know that."

Ivy felt his stare before she actually found where the chill was coming from. What was Will Dalhart doing following her around, going to the same steak house where she and Joyce were having a celebration? And who was that gorgeous woman with him? Good Lord, it was Felicia Withers, only the richest woman in all of Dallas. And was that an engagement ring on her finger? Well, it damn sure was a sight bigger than the one Will had bought for her when he proposed. But then it was Sonny who'd proposed to her; it was Will who'd asked Felicia to marry him. Ivy wondered if he'd been engaged to Felicia when he proposed to her. What a tangled mess. One thing for sure. She and Joyce were not turning tail and running away. There was no way Sonny . . . Will . . . was exercising that much power over her.

"This will be fine, thank you," she said to the waiter as he seated them. Her back and Will's were so close together she could have scooted her chair back six inches and felt the heat from his neck.

"Is that you Ivy?" Felicia raised her voice just a bit. "How wonderful to see you again. Imagine running into you in Austin. First Dallas and now here."

Ivy had no recourse but to turn around and acknowledge Felicia. "Hello, Felicia and you, too, Will. Imagine running into you two here."

"I'm engaged. Going to have a huge wedding and a house full of kids," Felicia held up her ring.

"It's lovely. Is that the Hope diamond? Hope you are very happy," Ivy said, her heart falling to the floor and shattering into hundreds of jagged pieces.

"No, I told him to buy me the Hope, but he couldn't get the owner to sell, could he, Will?" She asked, trying to draw Will into the conversation so he'd get that horrid scowl off his face.

"No, he couldn't," Will said. "We'd best order, now, darlin'. You said you were starving and I'm told they make the best rare steaks in the world right here."

"We already discussed that. It can't be better than Daddy's steaks he makes on the grill, but the company might be alright. Nice to see you, Ivy. Good luck with the new business and all," she said with a wave of her diamond as she went back to the menu.

"I didn't know," Joyce mouthed silently.

"It's okay," Ivy mouthed back. "I'll have the cheese plate with fresh fruit appetizer," she told the man who waited for their order.

"And we'll have a double order of breaded Brie with extra jalapeno jelly and sliced apples, while we wait on salads. We'll both have the Fleming Salad," Felicia said. "I know you well enough to know that'd be the one you like best," she winked at Will who still looked like a tornado about to tear up half of south Texas.

"That's right, darlin'," he grumbled.

"Then I'll have the warm spinach and mushroom salad," Ivy said through gritted teeth to her waiter. She'd eat every bite of it too. Will Dalhart was not going to have one single ounce of power over her.

"And I want a sixteen ounce ribeye, rare. Matter of fact, shoot the steer between the eyes, slap it in the skillet long enough to get the moo out, and bring it to me, and an order of onion rings," Felicia said.

Good! Onion rings. I hope he tastes them when he kisses her goodnight and thinks of the Strawberry Moon the whole time, Ivy thought, still feeling the negative vibes from his back.

"I want the petit filet mignon with a baked potato. Extra butter and sour cream," Ivy said.

"How would you like that cooked ma'am?" The waiter asked.

"Medium. Leave me lots of pink but no red," she said.

"And you ma'am," he asked Joyce.

"Just make it double. Whatever she said is fine," Joyce said. "And we'd like a bottle of wine from your reserve list. *Chateau La Gomerie.*"

"Oh, I forgot wine. Glad I overheard you two talking about it," Felicia motioned with a hand toward Ivy. "A bottle of *Ferrari Carano.*"

"And you sir?" Their waiter looked at him.

"The lady knows my tastes very well. I'll have what she ordered also. Only a baked potato instead of onion rings," he said.

"Excuse me. I'm going to the ladies room and get my composure glued back on firmly. Go ahead with the appetizers if I'm not back," Ivy whispered to Joyce.

"If you run out on me, I will quit without notice tomorrow morning," Joyce whispered back.

"Wouldn't think of it. No one has that kind of power over me," she said.

A few minutes later she leaned against the backside of the powder room door and sighed. Why had Will Dalhart brought his fiancée to the very restaurant she and Joyce had chosen? Why? Why? Why? Fate might, just might have put them together in Davis, Oklahoma. Those silly wagers played a part in that measure of fate. But it was asking too much to believe fate would bring them to the same restaurant too. No, Will had deliberately found out their plans and made arrangements to be there so she would see him with his intended. So it would close the issue of Sonny and Cameo forever and ever.

"Well consider it closed, Tonto. The Indian and the lightning bug princess are dead as of right now," she took a deep breath and opened the door, only to run right into Will as he came out of the men's room.

"Cameo?" He pushed her back away from his chest.

"So sorry. I wasn't watching where I was going, and as you well know, I'm a bit on the clumsy side. Forgive me," she said primly.

"Consider it done," he stepped aside and let her lead the way back to the tables.

Princess nothing, he thought. *She's no princess. She's the full fledged queen. The ice queen of the whole state of Texas. How did cold old Ivy Marshall ever turn into that sweet waitress who stole my heart? That should definitely go on the television as an unsolved mystery.*

Chapter Thirteen

Ivy and Will opened their apartment doors at the same time the next morning. She pushed the button for the elevator and they waited in strained silence, neither of them saying a word. Tension followed them inside the mirrored walls where Ivy looked at the ceiling and vowed to have the mirrors removed as soon as possible. He trailed after her into her office for their morning meeting of minds.

Once inside the office, she became a business woman of the first degree and caliber. Though not warm or friendly, she could discuss every facet of drilling, giving her ideas on the next steps the corporation should take and what they should expect financially. He impressed her with his knowledge of the financial end of the spectrum as much as she had bowled him over with her intelligence. At the end of the half hour allowed for their meeting, he told her that the next day should be in his office.

"We'll take turns so the staff will see us cooperating," he suggested.

"That will be fine," she agreed.

He left with a mere nod of the head. Once he was in the elevator, she laid her head on her desk and tried to make some kind of sense of the feelings ripping up her insides. That's the way Joyce found her ten minutes later.

"Hey, boss lady, you got a headache or are you dead?" She asked, throwing a morning paper on the desk.

"I'm dead," Ivy mumbled. "What is this?" She raised her head enough to see an article circled in red.

"Thought you might like to see the morning gossip section of the newspaper," Joyce grinned.

" 'Both of the vice presidents of the newest and biggest merging of oil companies in the state of Texas were out and about last night. Ivy Marshall, in the company of her newly engaged assistant, Joyce Walters, was seen at The Steak House. Also, at the same restaurant, by chance perhaps, Will Dalhart was seen with Felicia Withers, and she was sporting a diamond as big as a hen's egg. No big surprise there. They've been best friends for years,' " Ivy read aloud. "Well, tell us something we don't know, Miss Gossip Column editor."

"Just thought you'd like to see it," Joyce said. "You are now among the celebrities. Getting your name in the gossip column and all. Next thing you know you'll be dodging the paparazzi."

"Sure I will," Ivy shook her head. "Where'd you get this?"

"Everyone in the building gets one put on their desk

every morning," Joyce said. "I found that one in the lounge on our floor."

"Can you find me about a dozen or more?" Ivy asked. It was a crazy sophomoric idea, one no thirty year old vice president of a big oil company would think about actually doing. It was juvenile. Childish beyond words.

She was going to do it!

"Sure. Must be twenty or more laying around this floor alone," she said. "And I've got a list ready for you to look at. When do you want to begin interviews for my replacement?"

"Not today," Ivy said. That was an adult, mature decision. She didn't have time for such things today. "Just gather up every page you can find that has that gossip column on it."

At five o'clock that evening most of the employees went home. She always worked until six, getting more done in the last hour most days than she did in the previous eight. But that day she stayed behind her desk until eight thirty. If Will had another dinner date with his precious Felicia, then she didn't want to be anywhere near the elevators when he left or returned.

She rode up to her apartment in solitude, checking out her own reflection in every angle in the mirrors. She set her briefcase beside the door and fished around in her purse for her key. It was usually right there in the side pocket. She dug deeper and stuck her finger on the corner of a pair of fingernail clippers. The purse landed on the floor. Her finger went straight to her mouth. And Will Dalhart opened the door to his apartment.

"Troubles?" He asked.

"No," she said bending down to pick up all the items from her purse that were lying all over the place.

"I forgot my briefcase," he felt impelled to explain, though he didn't know why. "Thought I'd run back down and get it so I could go over a few more files this evening before bedtime."

"Oh, I thought maybe you were setting a new style there. Going out to dinner with Miss Withers in your pajama bottoms," she said.

"Don't be so catty, Ivy," he stepped inside the waiting elevator.

"Pardon me. That was a bit rude. Of course, you wouldn't be going out with your sweet darlin' in pajama bottoms," she said, slinging open her door and disappearing inside her apartment before he had time to say another word.

At least she knew where he would be all evening.

The next morning at five minutes until nine they opened their doors at the same time. Without a word, he pushed the button for the elevator. When the doors opened he almost dropped his briefcase. The mirrors were covered with newspaper. He cut his eyes around at Ivy, who stepped inside the elevator as if nothing had changed. He read the article circled in red, then realized all the pages were the same. What an ultimately childish thing to do. *Even more childish than playing with water hoses?* His conscience chided.

He fought back the first real grin he'd felt in two days. Ivy Marshall was jealous. Pea green jealousy oozed out of her with every strip of tape holding up that ridiculous article. She thought he'd given Felicia that diamond and she was jealous. He almost whistled as he got off the elevator on his floor and led the way to his office.

Half an hour later she marched out of his office, took every piece of newspaper off the mirrors on her way back up to the third floor, and danced a little two step jig before she got off the elevator. The look on his face was priceless when he read that article. Absolutely priceless. What would Miss Felicia Withers think of her fiancé if she knew he'd proposed to another woman, a common old waitress who worked at the Strawberry Moon Cafe? Maybe Ivy would just call the gossip editor later that day and drop that bit of information, anonymously of course, into her voice mail.

She and Joyce poured over big, thick wedding books that evening after work. Ivy ordered pizzas delivered and they narrowed the dress down to only one of twenty five. Now they had to find out where the bridal shops were in Austin and do some serious shopping. In one book they found a picture of the perfect dress for Ivy. A hunter green with a slit up the side of the long slim skirt, but it didn't have a plunging neckline. Joyce decided on Calla lilies for the bouquets after Ivy said she refused to carry one of those round ball looking nosegays.

It was well past midnight when Ivy called down to the door man and had him bring the company car around to take Joyce to her apartment a mile or so away. If Will could use it to carry his women to dinner, then she could use it for her own purposes, too, by golly.

The next morning at the appointed time, she and Will opened the doors into the hallway and stepped out at the same time. She pushed the button. Apparently if they were to meet in her office, then protocol said she'd call for the elevator. If they were to meet in his office then he could push the button. He looked entirely too happy that morning. Not unlike he did the morning they were in church at the tiny chapel on the side of the mountain at Turner Falls. A wicked little smile even played at the corners of the mouth she'd kissed how many times? Once. Twice. A dozen times the night he proposed.

The doors opened and newspapers covered the mirrors.

But she'd taken them all down right after he'd seen the article. How did they get back up there? She went to her corner at the far left back side of the elevator and tried to ignore them. But how could she? They weren't the same news articles.

Pictures of Felicia were plastered everywhere. Felicia and some man with premature gray hair. Fit looking fellow, but evidently gray even in black and white newspaper copy. Must be her father, Ivy thought as she let her eyes take in the one closest to her. Then she read the headline and scanned the article. Felicia Withers and Ray Baldry announce their engagement. Wedding planned at Christmas. Right above the picture was the date of the newspaper. One from Dallas. Two weeks before. While Will was still play acting at being Sonny Johnson, the cook at the Moon.

Ivy didn't know whether to dance a jig, grab Will and plant a passionate kiss on his lips, or pretend the walls of the elevator were still covered in mirrors. Childish as both stunts were she felt like singing and wished she had a lemon to suck on so she wouldn't be smiling when they discussed the day's business.

Neither of them quite knew how to breakout of the mold they'd set the past three days so they didn't try. Business was business. They discussed. They argued. They compromised and then he went to his office. When he was out of sight, she giggled. He chuckled as he removed the newspapers, wishing he'd left a strategically placed mirror so he could have seen her face when she realized he hadn't bought that rock on Felicia's left hand.

"Gossip column goofed," Joyce said as she carried two cups of coffee into Ivy's office. "Retraction today. Says that Felicia is engaged to some multi-billionaire and they're planning a Christmas wedding. Goes on to say that Felicia and Will are best friends and he's going to be her attendant at the wedding. How's that? He's going to be a maid of honor and so are you. Think he'd like to save a few dollars and borrow your dress?"

"Oh, no, he'll look much better in pink ruffles," Ivy laughed.

"And is that a real smile I see? I'd have shot the witch at the restaurant if I'd known you wanted Will to be a single man," Joyce said.

"I don't care if he's single or not. I just didn't want to be the ugly duckling that he proposed to on a bet when he was really engaged to another woman," she said.

"He can propose to you on a bet, but not if he's engaged? That don't make a bit of sense, Ivy," Joyce shook her head. "Don't have time to go into all that means, though. Tuck up your hair, darlin', and reapply your lipstick. You've got a meeting with some of those folks that need a translator in about ten minutes. Conference room. Will Dalhart and four board members. It's your first big meeting as the VP so look beautiful. Ugly duckling! Where do you get such silly notions?"

Ivy and Will presented a united front to the entourage. Instead of how many heads of lettuce they needed to purchase, they held their ground on how much per barrel their oil would cost. Instead of taking orders and cooking hamburgers, they shared a catered meal in a conference room with six important men and a translator. By lunch time they'd reached an agreement satisfactory to both parties. Ivy went back up to her office where Joyce had two interviews waiting and fifteen calls she needed to return.

She asked for half an hour to go over the two resumes and almost wept when she realized that her friend really was leaving. At the end of the day, she and Joyce had a conference and called in the young man who Joyce had already recommended. He was efficient, twenty nine years old, held a master's degree in business, had worked for the Houston company since graduation, was married, thus stable, and had ambition pouring out his pores. Ivy promoted him to junior associate and put him to work as of the next morning working with Joyce to learn her job.

"As if he could learn everything you do in five weeks," Ivy said when he'd walked on air out of the room. "You're more than just an associate and you know it."

"Of course he can. Got to admit something, though. I like Thomas. He's the best in the lot for the job. But I wanted a man to replace me. I don't want some other hussy coming in here and taking over my spot as your best friend. Thomas can do everything I do and more business wise. That's as much as I want him to do. I want you to have to call me when you do something stupid like paper the walls of the elevator with newspaper, or when you date a geek and need to talk about it. I'll give up my job as your associate. I won't give up my other position in your life without a fight, though," Joyce said.

Ivy hugged her. "Never," she promised.

"I know," Joyce sniffled. "But I'm just making sure. We've been friends for twenty four years and that's too much investment to see get washed down the drain by some brown nosing little twit who will never know you like I do."

"Never happen," Ivy swallowed hard.

She still had a lump in her throat when she rode the mirrored elevator up to the top floor. She opened her apartment door without dropping either her purse or briefcase and took time to stare at the closed door across the hallway from her door. Just because Felicia wasn't the one for him, didn't mean Ivy Marshall was. Maybe Sonny Johnson and Cameo Johnson had a chance, but not Ivy and Will.

Somethings were simply impossible.

Chapter Fourteen

The whole first floor lobby was decorated beautifully in white and shades of green. The cool breezes from the air-conditioning were a contrast from the hot September wind blowing outside in Austin, Texas that evening. The party, a catered affair with finger foods and a champagne fountain, had been scheduled immediately after work. Joyce had been misty-eyed all day, but Cyrus had flown down for the going away festivities and, when she saw him, Ivy could see that they really were in love.

Two eight foot tables draped in white satin held wrapped wedding gifts. Joyce would be missed sorely. Not merely for her office expertise, but for her smile, her attitude, and, for Ivy, her undying friendship. Ivy wondered if she'd ever find anyone who'd make her eyes light up like Cyrus did Joyce's. She had once as Cameo Johnson, but that was just a character on a stage. It wasn't real life or real people. She'd been the heroine in a movie where everything didn't always have a happy ending. She certainly hadn't been the heroine in one of her big romance books. If that had been the case, she wouldn't have had to wear glasses in the first place. She would have been born beautiful and perfect and the hero would have had to fight desire every waking moment just to keep his hands away from her and his lips from hers.

She hid behind an enormous potted plant and smiled at her own over active imagination. Come Monday morning, Thomas would be in Joyce's office. Life went on no matter what her name . . . Cameo or Ivy. But both of them, Cameo and Ivy, were jealous right at that moment. Cyrus stayed glued to Joyce's side, touching her arm when he talked as if he were afraid she'd disappear in a wisp of hot summer air. Joyce whispered something in his ear that made him blush and then kissed him on the cheek.

The man wasn't made of the stuff on the front of a romance book. He'd never be Fabio, but there was something about him in those twinkling blue eyes when he looked at Joyce that just plumb melted Ivy's heart. He adored her. Quite literally. Even though he was a bit on the gaunt side and didn't fill out his shirt like Will did; even though his face was a study of sharp angles and not oval with a sexy mouth like Will's; even all things considered, if someone would look at Ivy like that she wouldn't care what he looked like or how much money he had.

Sonny looked at you like that the night he proposed, her conscience pricked her heart.

"Yeah, right. He's a good actor as well as being handsome," she mumbled.

"Who you talking to, Miss Ivy?" Marvin joined her behind the plant. "You hiding out? Me too. Too many people for this old door man. I like 'em one at a time. Coming in or going out. Not all gathered up together, making noise and talking. Food is good though."

"You said it in a nutshell," Ivy raised her glass in a toast to him.

He clicked his with hers. "Got tea in mine. Never was one much for that champagne stuff. Tastes like weak beer if you ask me, and costs twice as much money as a good cold can of Coors. Not that I'd be drinking on the job, but a man does enjoy a good cold one on a hot summer evening when he gets home."

"I guess they do. Got a confession to make, Marvin," she whispered. "This is tea too. I don't like the champagne either. Sweet punch is more my style."

A wide grin split Marvin's chubby baby face. "See some folks parking at the curb. Guess I'd better do my job. Someday I'll expect to be drinkin' a bit of tea at yours and Mr. Dalhart's weddin' party."

She was tongue tied, speechless, unable to utter a word at such a preposterous idea. Marvin better not wait until that day to drink another glass of tea or his round baby face would go slack and he'd drop dead of dehydration.

"No hidin'," Red grabbed her from behind, practically making her drop her champagne flute filled with tea. "What's the prettiest girl at the whole shindig doing hugging the wall behind a flower?"

"You are prejudiced because I'm your only offspring and you're seeing all this wedding stuff and thinking grandbabies. It ain't damn likely," she grinned at him, letting him pull her out into the middle of the crowd.

"That's my line and don't you be using it lightly. That'd be a sin, my child. Kind of like the eleventh commandment. Do not take thy earthly father's sayings in vain," Red chuckled.

"Is that a storm cloud I see in the distance, Daddy? Could be you'll be dodging lightning bolts talking like that," she laughed with him.

"So the first few weeks have gone smooth as a new baby's behind, have they?" He asked.

"There you go again. Does everything have to do with babies when you are around me?" She asked.

"Not everything. Right now I want to know if my oil wells are producing and making me richer than old Midas," Red sipped his champagne.

"Yes, Daddy, not that you wouldn't make Midas look like a pauper anyway. But the business merged smoothly. You and John did a fine job of setting the foundation and getting the wheels running before you turned it over to a waitress and a fry cook," she patted his arm and let Joyce pull her away into a group of woman.

"What's the dress look like?" Someone asked.

"Oh, it's heavenly. No train though. We've decided on an outside wedding. Right out in the middle of the parking lot at Turner Falls Park. There will be arches and candles with hurricane lamp shades to keep the wind from blowing them out. Flowers everywhere, and anyway, I didn't want to drag a train around all evening on concrete and freshly mowed grass," Joyce said.

"Outside. What if it rains?" Another asked.

"Shhhh," Joyce shushed such an idea. "I'm not supposed to know," she whispered conspiratorially. "But I think Cyrus has paid someone," she rolled her eyes toward the ceiling, "to keep the rain clouds at bay. At least over the town of Davis for the whole day and evening."

The women snickered and Ivy checked out the window to make sure there were no lightning bolts dashing around. If one flashed, she intended to get as far away from her father and Joyce as possible.

She wandered back toward the safety of her potted plant only to find Will standing in front of it. "That's my place," she said then realized how silly it sounded.

"I was here first. Want to go outside and have a water fight to see who wins the honor of having the big plant to hide behind?" He asked.

"No past, Will," she reminded him.

"That was Sonny's idea. Not Will's. Will wants to talk about the past and the future. He likes both as well as the present," he said.

She watched his mouth as he talked. If she ever looked into his eyes, she'd for sure drag him behind the plant and throw herself into his arms. Watching his mouth wasn't such a good idea either. Now all she wanted to do was kiss him. Talk about being the most unlucky-in-love woman ever to walk upon the face of the earth. She'd fallen for someone who'd never see past a waitress apron, who'd never trust her anymore than she'd trust him.

"Did you get that Caddy ordered?" He asked when she didn't comment on his attempt at conversation.

"Didn't hold Daddy to the wager. It would remind me of too much . . ." she stammered.

"Let's find a quieter place," he took her hand.

His touch caused tingles up Ivy's spine just as Sonny's had affected Cameo. She let him lead her toward the elevators without even looking over her shoulder to see who might be watching. His thumb worked in small circles on the soft skin between her thumb and forefinger. She thought she'd die if he didn't stop. She was a grown, mature woman, who hadn't just fallen off the turnip truck. He was going to take her up to his office and tell her that they had enjoyed a brief experience but that they should go on with their lives now and put it behind them. Ivy, the unlucky, didn't harbor even the faintest hope of one more kiss before it was over.

"Hey, hey," Joyce's high heeled shoes made a ratty-tap noise as she crossed the floor toward them. "Where are you two off to? Deserting my party so early?"

"No, we need to go over one more thing before the weekend," Will said. "We'll be back in a few minutes."

Proof positive to support her previous thoughts, Ivy told herself. It would only take a few minutes to say what he had to say and for her to agree. After all, what else could she do? Sense over-rode passion. Mind ruled heart. Luck was only for the young and beautiful.

"Well, I almost forgot something," Joyce said. "April finally got around to sending these to me. Found one in the blender addressed to you," she pulled a note from her small dinner purse and handed it to Will. "And one in the refrigerator addressed to you," she gave the other one to Ivy. "Sorry boss, I know you said you wanted both of them, but I think that constitutes mail fraud, or is it blender fraud? Anyway, you both got what was intended for you. Oh, in case you don't get back to the party, thanks for a wonderful going away shower. We'll see you at the wedding on Friday night, right?"

"Of course, I'll be the one in front by the bride carrying a Calla lily and wearing a green dress," Ivy's voice was only a little shaky. How on earth was she going to get that envelope back from him?

"And I'll be the one on the back row in a black suit, suffocating to death in the heat. An outside wedding, Joyce? In September?" He said.

"At least you won't be wearing pink ruffles like you'll be doing at Felicia's wedding," Joyce laughed. "There's your elevator. See you both Friday. Thanks again."

She was halfway across the room when the elevator doors closed.

Will had let go of her hand to take the note from Joyce and he didn't reach out to grab it again. He pushed a button and they rode in silence, like they always did. When the doors opened she was surprised to find herself on the top floor with his apartment door on one side of the hall and hers on the other.

"I figured we'd have this discussion in your office," she said weakly, still clutching the note and wishing there was some way she could open it without him seeing her.

"A wise waitress told me once that you don't mix pleasure and business. Our offices are for business," he said, leading her to a door at the end of the hall she'd always figured opened into a storage closet or an air conditioning unit.

"Come with me," he held out his hand and she took it. He led her through the narrow door and up a flight of steps, though a metal door, and out onto the roof. An old timey patchwork quilt was spread out in the middle of the concrete roof, the corners fluffed back by a strong wind that had picked up out of no where.

"Sit with me," he led her to the quilt and pulled her down beside him.

"What is this? Looks like you planned to bring a woman up here. Couldn't you find one willing?" She asked, then wished she could bite her tongue and take the words back. The man was making an honest effort at romance and she was throwing it back in his face. Or was he? Could be that he was just softening the blow to the little waitress's heart.

"You must be willing. You came with me," he said.

"Are you going to read your note?" She asked, ignoring the tone of his voice.

"Not just yet," he laid it to one side and she put hers on top of it. When he said what he had to say, she'd pick them both up and they'd be ashes before she went to bed that night.

"It was just a wager born out of pride," he began. "I had to prove to my father and to yours that I was made of as tough a shoe leather as they were. That I could go it on my own with a menial job. I see now why you didn't go shopping that day I played golf. You would have had to leave Murray County and I imagine most of our rules were the same. Stay in Murray County for the whole month so we couldn't run up to the big city and play on the weekends."

She nodded waiting for the final blow.

"Fate surely dealt us some strange cards. I don't believe in coincidence and I believe people make their own fate, but after more than a month of thinking this through, it's got to be fate because nothing else fits," he said.

"I know," she said barely above a whisper.

"Funny thing was, I thought it was the job and the town that I loved. I thought it was not being Will Dalhart with a big bank account women were interested in. I thought it was the laid back, even if hard, work-ing life that made me so happy," he tried to remember all the pretty words he'd written down that day when he planned to be up front and honest. They'd all flown over the top of the railing around the roof onto the sidewalk below.

"Guess you thought wrong, huh?" She had to clear her throat to get that much out.

"Yes, I did. I thought wrong. It wasn't all the job, or the town, or the friendly folks there. It was you that made me happy. You, Ivy," he said.

"Wow," she muttered. *Wow*, she frowned. *Wow?* No wonder she was unlucky in love. She didn't even know what to say when a man paid her the ultimate compliment.

Will drew her into his embrace. "Yes, wow. That sums up the way I feel. I've run from it. Tried to kill it. But it won't go away. You see, my crazy heart doesn't care if I'm Sonny and you are Cameo and we're hold-ing down the Strawberry Moon in Davis, or if I'm Will and you're Ivy and we're sharing the vice presidency of DH Enterprises. It just knows that I fell in love with you and I've got a second chance. I brought you up here to ask you if you'd be willing to put the past behind us and try again. This time I promise to never lie to you."

"Was that proposal a lie? Was it just to win the wager? Did you tell my father and yours that you'd talked a poor waitress into marrying you?" She asked, snuggling down deeper.

"I thought it was to win the wager. No, I did not tell our fathers about it. I couldn't. The Porsche and the horse weren't worth hurting you that much. Using you like that. Was it a lie? At the time, I thought it was. But looking back it was the most honest, heart felt thing I'd ever done. I'd fallen in love with you and in my heart wanted to marry you. But I couldn't. Not that you weren't good enough as Cameo. But I wasn't good enough. I'd lied to you and to bring you to Austin where you'd be uncomfortable in my world . . . I just couldn't. Not that I wouldn't, but that I couldn't. Does that make a bit of sense?"

"It will if you kiss me like you did on the porch that night and if you'll say those words again. My old heart must've been formed in the same mold as yours because it feels the same way. I'm not graceful. Always been the ugly duckling and I'm bossy as they come. I'll argue with you and I'll try to be a good wife," she said.

Using his fist to tip back her chin and look down into her face, he leaned forward and lit up the whole town of Austin as his mouth met hers in a passionate kiss. "Will you marry me? This time I'm asking for real. And I know exactly who and what you are Ivy Marshall, and I love you just the way you are."

"Yes, oh yes," she said.

"I don't have a ring tonight," he said. "But we'll go pick one out tomorrow."

"No, we won't. I want a wide gold wedding band with no fancy diamond on it. Plain. Like Momma's was. I don't want to be engaged to you Will Dalhart. I want to be married to you. And I know just the place," she told him, forgetting all about the notes the wind had picked up and blown away.

"Then name it darlin' and we'll fly there next weekend."

"Yes, we will," she said, leaning in for another kiss to seal the deal.

Chapter Fifteen

At eight o'clock that evening Midas himself couldn't have produced enough gold to purchase a breeze, but there wasn't a storm cloud in the sky. Not a single solitary one. The bride dressed in a large room with only a window unit to cool it on the other end of the building from the Trading Post. She giggled with Ivy as she put the halo of fresh peach colored roses in her blond hair and adjusted the flowing white ribbons so they'd float down her back. She slipped into her shoes, declared they were pinching her toes, and hoped the crowd would forgive her after the wedding ceremony when she changed into a pair of sandals for the reception.

"It's beautiful," Ivy told her. "The whole idea. Who would have thought a parking lot could be changed into such a lovely place. And the reception under those trees. Mercy, but there's enough food down there on those tables to feed Sherman's march to the sea, girl."

"The whole town is invited and if there's one thing I

know, it's that the folks in this town love a good spread. Good for business, you know, and besides, Cyrus knows everyone and is kin to half of them. I'll have to learn the family tree before I can say a word about anybody. April will have to help me," Joyce said.

"Just keep your mouth shut until you ask me," April grinned from a corner where she curled her youngest daughter's hair. "Be still. And be sure to drop the rose petals as you walk down the aisle. There's lots of them so don't be stingy. The basket is big and stuffed solid with them."

"Tell Ivy where you got all those lovely rose petals," Joyce said with half a giggle.

April blushed scarlet. "You weren't supposed to mention that."

"But I did. Since you can't, I will. Cover the girls' ears so they won't hear. Wouldn't do for them to know what their Momma did. She may have to build two houses in Mexico next year to atone for her sins," Joyce teased.

"Whisper," April said. "You girls come here and I'll sing you a song while Aunt Joyce tells secrets to her best friend. On your wedding day you get to tell secrets too," she said then sang, "Itsy Bitsy Spider," at the top of her lungs.

"Her husband, Jim, was married once before. Right out of high school and it lasted three months. Jane," Joyce said.

"Jane? The one at the church social. The holier-than-thou?" Ivy could scarcely believe her ears.

"That's the one. No one ever talks about it anymore, scarcely remembers it," Joyce said. "But somehow in all the melee of the wedding we forgot to order roses to tear apart for the girls to drop. I'm not a rose person. Love daisies, blue bonnets, and lilies much more as you well know. So anyway," Joyce nodded for April to begin another round of singing and lowered her voice to a whisper, her mouth only inches from Ivy's ear.

"We needed roses. The florist didn't have a single one. Had two funerals in town today, too, so they were low on any kind of flowers. Anyway April remembered all those lovely rose bushes in Jane's yard, and Jane is conveniently out of town all week so she doesn't have to be here tonight. She wouldn't want to be around April or Jim. So April stole into her yard this morning before daylight and stripped those rose bushes bare. We've got lots of petals for the girls to toss on the rice paper for me to tread, and Jane is coming home to rose bushes that I'm sure will get laid off on the grasshoppers."

Ivy laughed until her sides ached.

"You're going to ruin your make-up," Joyce said. "Stop it."

"I can't. That's too funny," Ivy got the hiccups.

"If you have the hiccups walking down the aisle before me, they'll think we've been drinking in here," Joyce giggled.

"April, it's too funny," Ivy looked at the woman who'd joined them in a case of nervous giggles.

"Seemed fitting and my sister needed roses," April said.

Suddenly everything went quiet as a tomb when they realized Joyce was crying. "Now look what you made me do. I got to thinking about walking on those roses and how we always said we'd have a double wedding and you don't even have a feller, and I'm getting married. I should have waited for you," she dabbed at her mascara with a tissue.

"Stop it right now. Think about the look on Jane's face and how you'll have to keep from laughing every time you see her in church," Ivy scolded.

"Thank goodness we won't be attending the same church as they do," Joyce bit her lip and the tears disappeared. "It is a funny story, isn't it?"

"Should go down in the wedding book," Ivy said.

"There's the music. They're seating the mothers. Cyrus's momma thinks I'm a gift from God. I didn't have the heart to tell her if I was then God was guilty of handing out gag gifts," Joyce said.

"Okay, ladies, it's showtime," April herded her two daughters to the door. "Me next and then you, Ivy. Joyce, don't you even look at us during the ceremony. Keep your eyes on Cyrus because if you glance my way or look down the aisle at those roses, I'll lose it."

"Yes, ma'am," Joyce nodded. "Now let's get this done. My honeymoon awaits and I for one do not intend to be late for that part of this hullabaloo."

The wedding would be the talk of the town for years to come. The reception was perfect. The bride and groom left in a shower of bird seed just after ten o'clock. The long white limousine had tin cans and old boots tied to the back and just married written across the back window in shoe polish. The crowd dispersed, a few at a time, finally clearing out completely sometime around eleven.

All but Will and Ivy, who sat on the steps of the little chapel and watched the end of a perfect day from afar. At eleven thirty, a man appeared at the bottom of the stairs. "Am I on time?" He asked.

"Exactly," Will said pulling Ivy up by the hand he held tightly.

"Witnesses?" The man asked.

"Whoever is left over there amongst the caterers will do fine," Ivy said. "Give me three minutes and I'll bring a couple up the stairs with me. Go wait in the chapel. Long as we get the marriage kiss done by midnight then Joyce and I will be married on the same day."

"The good Reverend and I will be there. I'll be at the front in a dark suit without the hot jacket," Will said.

"I think I might recognize you," she kissed him quickly on the cheek.

In less than five minutes two tired looking women took their seats on the front pew of the chapel. Ivy followed them inside and carried the bouquet she'd caught when Joyce threw it from the limo window.

"You sure you don't want to wait and at least have your father and mine at our wedding?" Will asked.

"No, just us. They can have a lavish reception for us. Whatever they want. But we'll be married and they won't be able to bet on who'll back out or anything else. Now it's showtime and these two lovely ladies have more work to do. Your quickest ceremony, please, sir."

"Yes, ma'am," the preacher opened his Bible and began.

In ten minutes the ladies had signed the papers and Ivy Cameo Elizabeth Marshall was Mrs. Will Dalhart. The preacher took the license with him, along with Joyce and Cyrus's, to file at the courthouse on Monday morning. Will and Ivy were left alone in the chapel.

He leaned forward and kissed her again. "Sure you want to honeymoon in a cabin right here in the falls? I could have the plane take us anywhere you want to go. I don't even have a wedding gift for you."

"You are my wedding gift, but if we want a souvenir to remember our two day honeymoon, then before we leave on Sunday we'll buy a dreamcatcher. Meant to do it that day we came to the park and I forgot. I'm very serious, Will Dalhart. This is where I want to be. I want to be your wife and honeymoon right here," she said. "You going to carry me all the way down the stairs?"

"No, but I will carry you over the threshold," he hugged her tightly to his chest, unable to believe she was really his.

"How do you propose we get across that low water bridge and to our cabin?" She asked, suddenly aware they were without any form of transportation. She'd come to Davis with Joyce in her Lexus. Will had flown up in the company plane which would take them both home early Monday morning. There had been plenty of vehicles before the wedding. Now that it was over, they were on their own.

"Slip off those shoes, pull up your dress tail, and we'll wade," he said. "We might be past thirty but we ain't old, Mrs. Dalhart."

"And we never will be," she looped her arms around his neck and demanded one more kiss. "But I'll always love you."

"And I'll always love you," he sealed the promise and the two of them sat down on the first pew to take off their shoes.